**He tried not to touch her, but he couldn't help but drag a single finger down the exposed part of her arm. As suspected, she shivered beneath his touch.**

"Giving in would mean I get to unleash the heat and passion that I know you keep hidden. Although I can't understand why you try to hide it."

She finally turned to him, lust reflected in her eyes. "You left out one key factor in your statement."

"Which is?"

Her eyes dropped to his lips and lingered there for a while before meeting his gaze. "You never asked me what I wanted. Whether or not I wanted you to act on your attraction or not. You didn't even ask me if I'm attracted to you, too."

Chemistry this strong couldn't be one-sided, so he sensed she was attracted to him, as well. Even so, he had to ask just to be sure. "Are you attracted to me, too?"

"A pretty obvious yes..."

When she turned forward in her seat again, he didn't miss the smile that crept across her face. He was sure this was one of those moments that he was supposed to speak and figure out if this conversation concluded with them agreeing to act on their attraction. Or them agreeing that they shouldn't. But he couldn't seem to find the right words, and apparently, neither could she.

Dear Reader,

When Autumn Dupree was initially introduced in *Enticing Winter*, I immediately knew that she was the perfect match for Ajay Reed. Autumn needed a hero who would take the time to understand her, and Ajay needed a heroine who would really challenge him.

Autumn and Ajay were one of my most favorite couples to write about. While writing their story, I became so wrapped up in the emotions of each character. Both Autumn and Ajay had very difficult past experiences, but sometimes, the best way to overcome adversity is to confide in the one person who may understand you more than anyone else.

Summer's story is next, and I'm really excited for that release. You will finally meet Summer in *Falling for Autumn*. In addition to being just as driven as her sisters, she's also just as feisty.

Much love,

*Sherelle*

authorsherellegreen@gmail.com
@sherellegreen

**Sherelle Green** is a Chicago native with a dynamic imagination and a passion for reading and writing. Her love for romance developed in high school after stumbling across a hot and steamy Harlequin novel. She instantly became an avid romance reader and decided to pursue an education in English and journalism. A true romantic, she believes in predestined romances, love at first sight and fairy-tale endings.

**Books by Sherelle Green**

**Harlequin Kimani Romance**

*A Tempting Proposal*
*If Only for Tonight*
*Red Velvet Kisses*
*Beautiful Surrender*
*Enticing Winter*
*Wrapped in Red* with Nana Malone
*Falling for Autumn*

Visit the Author Profile page at Harlequin.com for more titles.

This book is dedicated to the readers who enjoyed the Elite Events series so much that it inspired me to write this spin-off series. I hope you enjoy the Dupree sisters just as much as you enjoyed the women of Elite Events. Thank you so much for all your book love and support!


**Acknowledgments**

To my cousin Dennis, who not only gave me inspiration for Ajay's character, but Jaleen's character, as well! There is so much more to you than what meets the eye, and not only are you charismatic with a big heart, but you've had to overcome a lot of adversity to become the man you are today. Not only are you extremely family-oriented, but you make sure that those you love know that they can count on you when needed. Life will always throw us curveballs, and you prove that obstacles don't keep us down, but make us stronger. I'm so proud of you, and I can't wait to see what the future has in store.

# *Prologue*

*In order to win the love of a strong-minded man, he must feel challenged, and desire that woman so bad that it hurts.* Ajay Reed reflected a little more. He'd overheard an older man telling a group of twentysomething-year-old guys that statement one day. Even though it had been years since he'd heard it, the comment still stuck with him. He considered himself a determined man, but he'd come across enough women to know that he no longer enjoyed the thrill of the chase. He was simple. Easy to understand, if you knew what you were looking for.

When anyone asked, he always claimed that he liked his women as he liked his everyday life…uncomplicated. So he couldn't understand why he seemed to be mesmerized by the mouthy woman standing before him giving him a lecture on the menu for Inferno, his newest lounge. Autumn Dupree didn't know the definition of *uncomplicated.* She was the type of woman who always had an opinion about everything.

"I'm sorry, but can we back up this conversation?" Ajay said, motioning for her to slow down. "How did Taheim and Winter asking us to meet result in you questioning my menu?"

She tilted her head to the side as one of her hands went to her hip. "Since we're standing in your office in Inferno right now, this conversation hardly constitutes as irrelevant."

"Maybe according to you. But to me it seems very irrelevant, since I didn't ask for your opinion on the menu."

"Well, maybe you should have," she said with a snarky smile. "I just don't understand why your menu doesn't offer any healthy options. You don't even list the calories of your dishes in the menu."

"That's because this is a lounge. Not a health club."

"What does that have to do with offering healthier options?"

He glanced at his watch, wondering what in the world was taking his brother, Taheim, and Autumn's sister Winter so long to arrive. He hadn't heard from Taheim in days, and before Autumn started arguing with him over the menu, she'd stated that she hadn't heard from Winter lately, either.

"Can we just talk about something else?" he offered. Anything that would get her to stop her rant about his choices in food.

"Like what?" she asked with a shrug.

"Like why my brother and your sister asked to meet with us after being MIA for almost a week."

"I have a theory..." She slightly worried her bottom lip and crossed her arms over her chest.

"And what might that be?" he asked when he realized she wasn't going to continue. Her eyes searched his face. He wished he knew why every time she observed him, he felt a slight kick in his gut. That was the main thing that irritated him about Autumn. He couldn't figure her out, and Ajay prided himself on being a good judge of character. After being burned by people one too many times, he'd spent years perfecting that trait. However, Autumn made him doubt his ability to read people. One minute she'd be giving her opinion on something he wished she wouldn't, and the next he'd catch her staring at him...trying to read his thoughts.

As much as she annoyed him at times, there was no denying her beauty. Her hazel almond-shaped eyes, full seductive lips and smooth milk-chocolate skin tone were definitely features that had instantly attracted him to her. No matter how much she tried to ignore their chemistry, sometimes he caught that look of interest in her eyes, too.

"Well, let's look at the facts," she said, uncrossing her arms. "Almost a week ago, Taheim made a declaration of love and proposed to Winter in front of everyone in attendance for the Inferno grand opening. Then, both Taheim and Winter disappeared, only sending us both texts to say they were fine. So we can assume they were in their own love cocoon."

"Okay, and those facts tell us what exactly?"

"If I had to bet money on it, I'd say they called us here to discuss the wedding. They probably set a date and I'm guessing this is their official 'will you be my best man and maid of honor' speech."

He was already shaking his head before she finished her statement. "There's no way they chose a date already. I know my brother. He's a careful thinker, and even though the proposal was a bit spontaneous for him, I'd bet he wants a long engagement. When he proposed, he hadn't even picked out a ring yet."

"I disagree," she replied, lifting an eyebrow.

"Big shocker."

"No, seriously, I've been paying close attention to them lately, and I figured if they did decide to tie the knot, I couldn't see Taheim wanting a long engagement. He's been waiting for weeks to tell anyone who would listen how much he loves Winter."

He took a moment to think about how Taheim had been lately. Autumn was right. He had been acting real territorial with Winter. But there was no way he was telling her that she was right.

"Well, if they did call us here for that, good for them. I haven't been a best man yet, so I'm ready to take on that honor." A quick observation proved that Autumn didn't share the same feelings as he did.

"What about you? Ever been a maid of honor before?"

"Um, no, and I don't really want to start now."

*What? Maybe I heard her wrong.* "Are you saying you don't want to be Winter's maid of honor?"

She waved him off. "Winter is already well aware I disagree with the whole wedding thing."

"I thought all women imagined their wedding day and being in their friends' or sisters' wedding party."

"Ha! That may be true for some women, but not for me. While I believe in marriage, I don't believe in the so-called wedding enterprise."

"Wedding enterprise?"

"Yeah, those suckers in the industry who convince you that in order to marry the person you love, you have to be willing to spend money unnecessarily. When in reality, they reap all the benefits. You know, like the venue, the florists, the cake designer. All those people get paid, but not the couple. Unless by some miracle they get back a ton of money in the form of a wedding gift."

He studied her eyes, detecting her seriousness about the matter. She talked with a lot of passion, he'd give her that. He remembered his brother telling him a few weeks ago that Autumn was one of those people who spoke only when she felt as if there was something she needed to say. He was sure Taheim was just repeating how Winter had described her, but since he'd met Autumn, he couldn't recall there ever being a time when she didn't have something to say.

And he had no idea why he wanted to hear more about her point of view on weddings, but he did. She wasn't like any woman he'd met before, and the old Ajay would have wanted to accept the unspoken dare to try to figure her out. Unfortunately, he'd changed a lot since then, so he'd have to pass on accepting the challenge.

"Aren't you friends with the founders of Elite Events Incorporated?" he asked. Ajay and Taheim had grown up with Imani, Cydney and Lexus, since their families were from the same neighborhood, and had quickly developed a friendship with Mya, as well. He was proud of the corporation the four women had built from the ground.

"Yes, but what do they have to do with anything?"

"Since they're event planners, they often plan weddings. And Lex is your cousin-in-law while Mya is your soon-to-be cousin-in-law."

She squinted her eyes in confusion. "Once again, not seeing the correlation here."

He wondered if she was being difficult on purpose or if she genuinely didn't see where he was going with his thoughts. "Doesn't that make them part of those groups of suckers you're referring to?"

"Ah, now I see what you're getting at," she said, nodding her head. "Simply put, the answer is yes. However, I'm not that biased to believe that all people in the industry are out to get your money. I happen to really respect Elite Events Incorporated and what the women have accomplished. Besides," she said with a shrug, "they are well aware of my views on the matter, just like my sister is."

"Unfortunately, anyone who knows you is well aware of your views," said a female voice coming from the office doorway.

Ajay turned to see Taheim and Winter enter the room looking as if they didn't have a care in the world. There was also no mistaking that huge rock on her finger.

"So, baby bro, I guess you really didn't waste any time getting a ring."

"Are you kidding me?" Taheim said, never disconnecting his hand with Winter's. "I couldn't wait to put this ring on her finger and let everyone know that she is mine. The sooner men know she's off the market, the better."

As the newly engaged couple shared an intimate kiss, Ajay glanced over at Autumn just in time to see her mouth *Told you.* She was mouthing something else after that, but he didn't catch the rest of her words. He was too busy admiring the way her lips moved. Pouty. Sensual. She must have noticed him staring, because she stopped moving her mouth and gave him an inquisitive look. He gave her a look right back as if to say, "Yes, I was looking. What are you going to do about it?"

"Did you hear what I just said?" Taheim asked, gaining back his attention.

"Sorry, what did you say?"

Taheim looked at Winter with a huge smile on his face. "We decided to get married next October."

"Wow, congrats, bro," Ajay said, leaning in for a hug. "That's great."

"Even better," Winter said with a squeal, "we've chosen to have a destination wedding in Bora Bora."

Ajay glanced over just in time to see Autumn slightly cringe at her statement. After what she'd just told him, he assumed she was probably thinking about all the unnecessary money the couple would spend on a destination wedding.

* * *

Autumn lightly squeezed the bridge of her nose, hoping that she was hearing her sister wrong. "That's less than a year away. Isn't that a bit soon for a wedding out of the country?"

Winter smiled. "What about saying congrats before you lecture me?"

"I'm sorry, sis." The last thing Autumn wanted Winter to think was that she wasn't happy about her engagement to Taheim. She walked over to give Winter a hug. "I'm so happy for you both and I think you're perfect for each other." Winter returned her hug while Taheim offered her a smile.

"So what made you both choose Bora Bora?"

Winter held Taheim's eyes the entire time she spoke. "Well, I really wanted a destination wedding."

"And I really wanted to get married someplace hot," Taheim added.

"I wanted only our closest friends and family in attendance."

"And I reminded her that even that number is larger than she may think."

*Oh, great, they're already finishing each other's sentences.* On one hand, Autumn found it adorable, and on the other, she was surprised their relationship had escalated so fast.

"Neither one of us likes things to just be ordinary, so we knew we wanted to have a different type of wedding."

"You mean different besides the fact that you want to have the wedding in Bora Bora?" Ajay asked.

"Oh, yeah," Winter responded. "We're talking different as in beach chic and sexy elegance complete with a masquerade beach theme and reception."

Autumn was sure her mouth dropped, although she honestly shouldn't be surprised. Winter was a free spirit who loved to make a statement, and judging by what she knew of Taheim, *making a statement* were his middle names.

"Can I ask how exactly you two came up with this wedding theme?"

"You could, sis, but I already know that any validation won't change the fact that although you're happy for us, you hate weddings."

"*Hate* is a strong word. I think *strongly dislike* is more accurate."

She heard Ajay huff, but refused to look in his direction. Being around him threw her off her game. Instead of sounding like an intelligent realist around Ajay, she came across as a babbling chatterbox.

"Autumn, despite how you feel, I want you by my side for my wedding." *Oh, no, here it goes.* "It wouldn't be the same if I didn't have my sister and best friend right beside me on my special day, so I got you this."

Trembling fingers accepted the teal-and-white box wrapped in a beautiful lace ribbon. She looked from the box to Winter, unable to keep from smiling after noticing the huge grin reflected on her sister's face. When she opened the box, there was a photo of them when they were teenagers.

"Do you remember when we took that?" Winter asked.

"Of course." It was the day after a lot of drama had happened with their parents and they had promised each other that if they found *true* love, they would be there for each other every step of the journey. When she lifted the photo, she noticed a custom wineglass and a small bottle of her favorite red wine with a note attached to it.

"You've already done a great job at helping me acknowledge my feelings for Taheim," Winter said as she watched Autumn read the card. "I need you by my side. I need you to be my maid of honor."

Autumn couldn't help the emotion she felt in her heart. "Of course I will, sis." As they hugged, she glanced over her shoulder in time to see Taheim ask Ajay to be his best man. After he agreed, Ajay caught her eye and for the first time tonight, her dislike for weddings wasn't her most prominent thought. Instead, she was trying to calculate approximately how much time the best man and maid of honor would have to spend together. Spending any amount of time with a man as handsome as Ajay was enough to make a woman like her lose her ability to think straight.

# *Chapter 1*

*Eight months later...*

*I need you to be by my side. I need you to be my maid of honor.* Autumn Dupree couldn't seem to forget her sister's words no matter how hard she tried.

"You must be so excited for your sister."

Autumn downed the rest of the champagne in her glass before facing the enthusiastic voice. "Of course I am," she replied through gritted teeth. "All this love, happiness and months of planning ahead for a single twenty-four-hour day. Who wouldn't be happy, right?" The perky woman blinked her eyes a few times before abruptly walking away.

"Maybe you can work on a stiff smile and refrain from the sarcasm until after the engagement party."

Autumn rolled her eyes at her friend and store manager of Bare Sophistication lingerie boutique, Danni Allison. "I refuse to pretend to believe in weddings when I don't."

"But you agreed to be the maid of honor, and in doing so, Winter expects you to at least pretend to be happy for her."

"I am happy for her." Autumn shifted from one leg to the other in frustration as she glanced around the crowded Reed family home. "But this is too much fuss for one freaking day. I mean, what's in the Chicago water we've been drinking, because since I moved here a few years ago, there have been more engagement parties than I can count. And we already had an engagement party for Winter and Taheim right after they were engaged months ago, so I don't even know what this is."

"Taheim's mom had a bunch of old college friends in town and she wanted to do something special for her soon-to-be daughter-in-law. Especially since a lot of people won't be going to Bora Bora for the wedding. Didn't you read the email I sent you?"

She turned up her eyebrows at Danni. "You know, studies show you only have thirty seconds to intrigue a reader, and that booklet of wedding stuff you sent me lost my interest within the first five seconds."

"You should have been the person putting that so-called booklet together. I'm just a bridesmaid."

"You're already aware that I've been hosting a lot of our Bare Sophistication masquerade lingerie parties while Taheim and Winter have been on tour showcasing all their designs from their own clothing and lingerie lines. You told me it wouldn't be a problem."

"It isn't a big deal, but at the very least, I expect you to read what I email you."

"Last I checked, fifteen percent of engagements are called off anyway, so I figured it would be a waste reading something that may not even be relevant in a few months."

"You're lucky I appreciate your snarky attitude," Mya Winters-Madden said as she approached the women with Lex Turner-Madden walking beside her. "Otherwise, I'd have some real issues with that statement."

Mya had married Autumn's cousin Malik Madden just last month—only three months after giving birth to a beautiful set of boy and girl fraternal twins, believing for months that they were only pregnant with one child. Lex had married Malik's brother, Micah, a year and a half ago. Growing up, she remembered conversations she'd had with Malik, Micah and Winter about how none of them were ever getting married. Boy, had the tables turned.

"Although I'm glad my cousins found such amazing women like the two of you, I still stand firm in my beliefs regarding weddings."

Lex laughed as she shook her head. "We wouldn't expect you to be anyone but yourself. Even so, Mya and I have both been in Winter's shoes, and it helps when you know that those close to you support your marriage."

"I'll support their marriage wholeheartedly. It's weddings that..."

"We know, we know," Danni interrupted. "It's weddings that you dislike, not the idea of marriage."

"Exactly." There wasn't anything she wouldn't do for Winter, but she still couldn't believe she'd actually agreed to be a pivotal part of this shindig. Weddings were superficial. If one did decide to take the plunge, she never understood why they didn't just go to a courthouse and save themselves the hassle of planning. However, she knew people were tired of hearing her talk about her view on weddings, so she had to do a better job of keeping her mouth shut.

"I'll try my best to show my support." Her voice didn't sound as believable as she hoped it would, but she really meant what she said. After a few more skeptical looks, they finally turned their focus to another topic. Out of all the people Autumn had met since moving to Chicago, Danni and the ladies of Elite Events Incorporated probably knew her better than most of the friends she had back in New York. Autumn wasn't an easy nut to crack. Oftentimes, it took people a while to understand her quirky personality. However, she'd decided long ago that it didn't matter if people didn't appreciate the type of person she was. As long as she knew who she was, that suited her just fine.

"Malik is the worst when it comes to changing diapers," Mya said. "He'll spend all day playing with the twins, but when it's time to change a diaper, he makes himself scarce."

Autumn laughed. "We weren't around babies much growing up, so maybe you need to teach him how."

"Oh, he knows how," Mya replied. "He just refuses to do so. Next time I get a whiff of a smelly diaper, I'm forcing him to change it."

All the women shared a laugh as they joined others in the bridal party. Glancing over at Winter, Autumn couldn't help but be proud of her sister. Their childhood had been anything but easy, and she couldn't recall ever seeing her sister so happy. The opening of their Chicago lingerie boutique, Bare Sophistication, came a close second. But even so, Winter had been sporting the biggest smile since accepting Taheim's marriage proposal.

As if she knew Autumn was thinking about her, Winter glanced over at her and smiled. Since they were only eleven months apart, they often knew what the other was thinking. Irish twins in more ways than one. It often drove their younger sister, Summer, crazy, but they couldn't help it. They shared a connection that was unexplainable.

"When is Summer flying in?"

"She should be here in a few weeks and will stay until the wedding."

"Great. Are we still meeting next week to discuss the other wedding events?" Danni asked.

"Yes, we're still on."

What Autumn didn't mention was that she needed Danni to be there. She'd managed to avoid planning any wedding duties alone with Ajay, but with the wedding eight weeks away, she would have to face the inevitable. It was crunch time, and she would be seeing more of Ajay whether she liked it or not.

A couple of months ago, Winter and Taheim had decided to plan a coed combined bridal, bachelorette and bachelor party in Chicago for their extended friends who wouldn't be able to attend the wedding. It was definitely a plan unlike any Autumn had heard before, but different worked for Winter and Taheim.

She was pulled from her thoughts when she heard the group share a laugh at something Mrs. Reed had been saying about Taheim as she called him and Winter to the front of the room. Autumn really liked Mrs. Reed. She was so unlike her own mom, and she was glad to see her and Winter's relationship blossom. Her sister needed a motherly figure after all their mom had put her through growing up.

When Taheim's sister, Kaya, took the stage, Autumn felt the hairs on her arms stick up. Even at thirty, almost thirty-one, she still got nervous about public speaking when she didn't know what to say.

"I'm going to step out for a bit," she whispered into Danni's ear when she caught Mrs. Reed looking her way. She knew what was coming next. It was the same thing that had happened during every prewedding event she'd attended for Winter and Taheim. Whoever started talking first to the attendees would make eye contact with the maid of honor, best man or any member of the bridal party so that others could share a few words, as well.

When she found a door leading to the beautiful outdoor garden that Taheim's mom had shown her months ago, she breathed a sigh of relief. Autumn excelled at discussing things such as her lingerie boutique or a good political debate. But when it came to discussing love, merriment and all that jazz, she always felt socially awkward. As if her forehead had the words *fish out of water* stamped across it. Since she had such a sour view on weddings, all wedding-related activities made her feel uncomfortable.

She glanced around in the darkness, looking for a nice spot to relax. The concrete bench next to a large oak tree and a dim light that illuminated part of the pond was perfect.

"Much better," she said when she sat down, kicked off her heels and lay on her back. Usually, she would worry about wrinkling her cute black dress or messing up the updo that had taken her a half hour to create. But in this case, lying on her back with her head tilted slightly more downward than her body was the only thing that helped her headache go away. It was something her dad had always done growing up to get rid of his headaches, and strangely enough, it worked for Autumn every time.

"Well, the view out here definitely just got better." The deep baritone voice caused her to sit upright on the bench as she glanced toward the tree. She thought about asking who was out there, but it was pointless. She knew that voice anywhere. It often appeared in her dreams, although she really wished it didn't.

She waited for Ajay to come from out of the darkness, and when he did, she was tempted to tell him to go back behind the tree. He was wearing a blazer, jeans and Timberland boots—the same attire he usually wore. As usual, he looked as sexy as ever.

She instantly squeezed her thighs tighter to try to ease the warmth. Every time she saw him, it was either his voice or his eyes that did the trick. *Thank goodness he's too far away for me to see his eyes.* He had one of those rare eye combinations that often changed colors depending on the weather. Normally, his eyes were light brown, but on more than one occasion when they'd gotten into a heated debate, the color deepened to a dark gray with a hint of a brown around them. That was something they had in common. Her eyes often changed between hazel and light brown depending on her mood.

"What are you doing out here?" he asked, walking closer to her.

She shrugged. "I assume the same thing as you. Escaping the party."

When he got closer to her, she moved her feet in case he wanted to sit down. His eyes lingered on her legs before he took a seat on the bench.

"Why are you out here?" she asked him in return. "To escape the party, right?"

He gave her a crooked smile. One that she hadn't seen before. "Yeah, you're right. Taheim and Winter have had so many prewedding events, I'm running out of things to say."

"You never seem tongue-tied when you speak at these things."

"Well, maybe that's only half the truth. Lately, my mind is preoccupied with other thoughts."

She wanted to know what else was on his mind, but

that was so unlike her. She usually didn't push people for more information. She chanced a glance at him and noticed the faraway look in his eyes. *Don't ask him about his thoughts. Don't ask him about his thoughts.*

"What other thoughts are preoccupying your mind?" *Crap. Big fail.*

Instead of responding to her, he looked her way, and she could have sworn that his eyes briefly dropped to her lips. He seemed as if he was going to answer, when Autumn heard someone yelling for them. She glanced toward the house, where the voice had come from.

"It's Taheim," Ajay supplied. "We better get back in there. Duty calls."

She nodded her head in agreement, still wondering what other thoughts were occupying his mind tonight. *Were his thoughts about a woman?* If so, why should she even care? They weren't exactly friends and they talked to one another only because they sort of had to. There were a million reasons why she shouldn't care, but at the moment, she couldn't think of even one.

They fell into step beside one another, and it wasn't until they were almost at the house that she realized this was one of the first times they hadn't argued about anything.

Ajay had no idea what Taheim's friend Jaleen Walker was saying, but he knew it didn't matter. Knowing Jaleen, it was probably just some random comment about a woman he'd hooked up with the night before.

Nope, Ajay didn't care at all. Not when he had more important things to think about. Such as why, when he had so much on his mind, he couldn't stop admiring the way Autumn was sipping her wine.

When she'd stepped outside to escape the party, he'd watched her until she made it to the bench. He couldn't take his eyes off her legs when she'd raised them to lie down. They were long and beautiful. He'd bet they'd look even better wrapped around his waist. In that moment, she'd seemed so approachable, unlike the woman who always got on him about the food he chose to place on the menu of his venues.

Lurking behind the tree without saying anything would have been creepy, so he'd decided the best thing to do was to make his presence known, even though he would have rather admired her in the darkness.

"Hey, man, did you hear anything I just said?"

He forced himself to stop looking at Autumn. "I'm sorry, what did you say?"

"I asked if I can meet with you over at Autumn's to discuss that bachelor-and-bachelorette-party combo event you all are planning. I was talking to Danni about it and she mentioned that she was meeting up to discuss it with Autumn, and I remember you had spoken about it, as well."

*Hmm, I didn't know Autumn had told Danni.* It was probably for the best because he didn't want to be left alone with her anyway. Whenever he was around Autumn lately, he seemed to want to do things so out of character, such as ask questions to learn more about her. He guessed they wouldn't agree on much anyway, so if Danni and Jaleen joined, more would get accomplished.

"Yeah, that's fine. We could use the help."

"Good," Jaleen said, taking a swig of his beer. "From the way you were just staring at Autumn, I thought you may tell me no to eliminate the competition."

"You aren't competition."

"Yeah, okay."

He took a sip of his bourbon on the rocks and resumed his original task of observing Autumn. "If you're thinking about hitting on Autumn, don't bother."

He could feel Jaleen smiling, but he kept his eyes focused on her. He knew even if they were attracted to one another, they would never cross that line. But Jaleen liked to screw anything in a skirt, so Ajay had no problem staking a claim on Autumn if that meant Jaleen wouldn't flirt with her.

## *Chapter 2*

Ajay glanced at his watch, wondering if maybe he'd gotten his days mixed up. He reached in his pocket and pulled out his iPhone to call Taheim. When he didn't answer, he decided to call Jaleen.

"Hey, man, are we still meeting at Taheim's tonight?" he asked when Jaleen answered.

"Yeah, as far as I know."

"The doorman let me up because I assume Taheim told him he was expecting me. But I rang the doorbell and knocked. He's not answering."

"Probably because Winter hasn't left for her sister's place yet. You know they've been inseparable lately. I'm surprised Taheim even offered to have poker night at his place now that Winter has moved in."

Ever since Ajay had walked in on Taheim and Winter

in a compromising position, he'd locked the spare key he had for his brother's place in his safe so he would need to use it only for emergencies.

"Come down to my place and I'll text Taheim so he can let us know when he's ready for poker night. I'll text the other guys, too, so they can just come to my place and chill out."

Jaleen lived in the same building as Taheim in a penthouse suite located in the separate wing of the luxury complex.

"Sounds good," he replied, already making his way to Jaleen's penthouse. When Jaleen and Taheim had both decided to stay in the same 244-unit building a few years ago, they'd tried to convince Ajay that he should stay there, as well. However, Ajay was more of a house man, not a condo person. His five-bedroom, three-bathroom home might be too much space for a bachelor, but he enjoyed having room to breathe and do whatever he wanted in the comfort of his home.

"Hey, man," Jaleen said as he opened the door and stepped aside for Ajay to walk in. "I already texted the other guys. We may just move poker night here instead."

"Works for me."

"Cool. Have you talked to Autumn today?"

He looked at Jaleen questioningly, not understanding why he randomly brought up Autumn.

"No. Why?"

"No reason," Jaleen replied with a smirk on his face. "I just need to make sure you don't try to hit on my future woman."

He'd known Jaleen long enough to know when he was up to something. Jaleen was always scheming and getting into other people's business. "Yo' woman? I thought I made myself clear the other day at the party."

"But I thought you weren't attracted to her?"

"I never said I wasn't attracted to her. I just told you not to hit on her."

"So you *are* attracted to her?"

"Why does it matter if I am or not?"

"Is that a yes?"

He laughed, trying to change the subject. "When did the other guys say they would get here?"

"I'll tell you right after you answer my question. I know you've been out of the game for a while…"

It was true that Ajay hadn't seriously dated anyone in a while, but in his line of work, women were constantly throwing themselves at him. Years ago, he was known for bedding one woman after the next, but he had always made it clear to them that he wasn't a relationship type of guy. It had only taken him getting burned a couple times to change his perspective on the opposite sex. He still enjoyed a woman's company every now and then, but at thirty-five, he needed more than a pretty face to make him stay around.

"It hasn't been that long." As the words left his mouth, he thought about the fact that he hadn't had sex in over four months. For an insatiable man like him, that was forever ago. When Jaleen continued to ride him about his lack of dating women lately, he decided to give in and answer the question Jaleen really wanted to know.

"Well, yeah, Autumn is an attractive woman, so naturally I'm drawn to her. But the reason I told you to back off is for her own good, not mine. If I wanted to pursue Autumn, she'd know it and so would you and any other guy interested in her."

Jaleen was smiling from ear to ear by the time they entered the entertainment room. Ajay stopped dead in his tracks at the sight of Autumn sitting on a bar stool sipping a cocktail. One look at her face and he'd known that she had overheard part of the conversation. He cut his eyes at Jaleen, who simply turned his shoulders in a shrug.

"Hello, Autumn," he said as he approached her. "Surprised to see you here."

She gave him a soft smile. "Winter asked me to pick her up so that she wouldn't have to find a place to park her car when she came over. When I got here, she texted me that she needed another hour."

He nodded his head in understanding, but wished he could wipe that smirk off Jaleen's face. Jaleen was trying to work in casual conversation by asking Ajay about the nightclubs and bars that he owned in the Chicagoland area and asking Autumn about her lingerie boutique and the masquerade lingerie events that were quickly gaining more exposure. They both supplied simple two- or three-word answers, and a quick study of Autumn's demeanor proved that his earlier assumption was right. She'd definitely heard part of their conversation. They'd been in the same room for over five minutes and she hadn't even gotten mouthy with him yet. Even stranger, he actually missed her sassiness.

"Autumn, can I get you anything else?" Jaleen asked as he slid beside her on an adjacent stool.

"No, I'm fine."

"Yes, you are." The double meaning of Jaleen's words didn't go unnoticed by Ajay.

"Are you always this flirty?" she asked, taking a sip of her drink. The way her mouth curled around the glass was distracting. He'd been thinking about her lips way too much lately.

"Only around attractive women." Ajay snorted at Jaleen's lame attempt at flirting. Jaleen used every line in the book, and to this day, he never understood why it actually worked on most women. Fortunately, it didn't seem to be working on Autumn.

When a buzzer sounded indicating that someone wanted to be let up to Jaleen's condo, Ajay was left alone with her. When seconds ticked into minutes and Jaleen still hadn't returned, the awkwardness grew. Ajay racked his brain to try to think of something to talk about but came up short. *This is a shame. Thirty-five years old and I'm acting as if I don't have game.* Not that he wanted to spit game at Autumn. Nor did he want to notice that the woman made jeans and a T-shirt look as sexy as if she were wearing a short, tight dress.

Even though they were both trying to focus on random things around the room, their eyes found each other. He couldn't quite read the look in her eyes, but there was no mistaking the change of energy in the space.

"Interesting," she said, her eyes still locked to his.

"What's interesting?"

"I think I'd rather keep it to myself."

Now he really wanted to know. "Whatever you tell me, I won't say a word."

"If I don't tell you, it guarantees you won't say a word because you won't know anything. It's common knowledge that people typically can't hold secrets."

"I've always been great at keeping secrets." He didn't even notice that he was walking closer to her until he was only a couple of feet away. Being this near to her, he was able to see things that he hadn't from a distance. He wished he could free her hair of that neat ponytail. It fit her personality. Organized. Uptight at times. With the exception of a few stray hairs, nothing was out of place. But he had a feeling that deep down, there was a side of Autumn that she rarely released. A side that wasn't tame or disciplined.

"What are you thinking about?"

His lips curled to the side in a smirk. "I'll tell you exactly what I'm thinking if you tell me your secret." When she remained quiet, he continued, "Or are you too scared of what I may think if you tell me your secret?"

She didn't answer at first and he felt as if he was holding his breath for her answer. Squinting her eyes together, she leaned a little closer to him. "Your pupils are changing colors," she said softly.

"That happens on occasion."

"I know. And that's part of the reason why I won't tell you my secret."

He scrunched his forehead in confusion. "I don't understand."

"When I don't understand something, I study it to try to figure it out."

"Am I to assume I'm your latest study?"

"That's not what I'm saying."

"Are you saying I should be studying you, then?"

"Certain things about you do pique my curiosity," she responded. "So to answer your first question, I'm not too scared of what you may think."

"Then, why can't you tell me your secret?"

At the sound of footsteps, she lowered her voice. "I can't tell you my secret because I'm worried of what you may do."

As Jaleen entered followed by a couple of the guys, Ajay was still contemplating Autumn's words. She may not have wanted to tell him the secret, but she'd revealed what type of secret it was without indulging the information completely. What she didn't understand about him was that her statement wasn't going to make him stop asking. If anything, he wanted to know what she was hiding even more.

A bunch of arrogant males vying for her attention she could handle, but there was one hot-blooded male in the room who was occupying all of her thoughts. She could kill Winter for pushing back their meeting time. At least she felt a little more like her normal self. Now all she needed to do was convince Luke, one of Taheim's groomsmen, to take a few steps out of her personal space.

"Have I told you how beautiful you look tonight?"

She sighed. Just like Jaleen, Luke was attractive.

Both men could have their pick of women in Chicago. The main reason Autumn didn't entertain their flirtatious ways was the muscular man observing her in the corner of the room sporting tattoos so sexy she wished she could trace them with her tongue.

Since it was mid-August, the fall season was right around the corner and she had gotten a chance to see Ajay's bare, muscular arms only a few times. He was always wearing some type of blazer or long-sleeved shirt despite the heat. His urban style wasn't something she usually found attractive, but Ajay was giving a whole new meaning to the term *fashionable street wear.*

He was rough around the edges, but smooth on the corners. A definite charmer from what she could tell, but he wasn't the type of man who had to try to get attention. Women were just drawn to him. Unlike Jaleen and Luke, he wasn't in your face, but rather the silent assassin who struck when you least expected it. He seemed like a simple guy, but he had layers, and damn her curiosity for wanting to see what other coatings he had.

"So tell me, Autumn, is there someone special in your life?"

"No, there isn't. What about you?"

"No one as mesmerizing as you."

*Oh, Lord, I don't know how much more of this I can take. Strike one.* She was all for a little harmless flirting, but this was becoming a little too much.

"So tell me, Luke, what is so mesmerizing about me?"

"That's easy," he said with his eyes smiling. "I'm mesmerized by your beauty."

"Okay, what else?"

He leaned a little closer to her and she was tempted to tell him to lay off the cologne next time. "And your eyes are beautiful."

"Anything not related to my looks?"

"I'm blinded by your beauty, but mesmerized by your entire package."

*Strike two.* She wondered why men thought complimenting a woman's entire package was a good thing. He could think it. But to say it?

"My package? All physical, or is there something about my personality that's included in that?"

"Of course there is, sweetheart." He flicked her chin with his finger and she barely heard whatever answer he gave. *Strike three. Do not touch me unless I give you the signal to do so.* She definitely had not given him the signal. She never was the touchy-feely type.

Her phone buzzed and she read the text from Winter saying that she was ready. She glanced back at Luke, wondering if he had any idea that her sister's text had just saved him from a few of her choice words. Since she still had to see Luke for all the wedding stuff, she was glad she'd gotten the message.

"I have to go," she said, standing up from the stool.

"We should go out sometime."

"No, thanks."

"Maybe you want to reconsider." He gave her what she assumed was his sexy face. She wasn't feeling it.

"Hmm, no need. My answer will still be no. You, on the other hand, will find some other poor soul to spit lines to." She laughed to mask the jab.

"You'll be sorry," he yelled after her playfully.

"Doubt it." She was glad he didn't seem bitter about it. Probably the only thing about him that she actually liked was that he didn't get bent out of shape too easily.

She said her goodbyes to the entire room, trying to flee Jaleen's condo before any of the guys decided they wanted to flirt some more. Right before she was out of the room, she noticed Ajay glance at his phone and assumed he'd just heard from Taheim. He glanced at her and smiled. She thought about the words she'd heard him say when he was talking to Jaleen. On one hand, she was glad that he found her attractive but wasn't acting on it. On the other hand, she was dying to know what on earth was making him hold back.

# *Chapter 3*

Of all the workouts her sister had decided to try before the wedding, hot yoga was by far Autumn's favorite.

"That's it, ladies and gentleman. Take a deep breath and exhale."

Autumn maintained her tree pose as she concentrated on her breathing and listened to the instructor. As usual, she had to ignore the grunts from Danni and Winter, who didn't enjoy hot yoga nearly as much as she did. She wasn't sure if it was the fact that the temperature in the room was currently set to ninety degrees, or if it was because both the women liked to chat when they worked out, and yoga definitely did not allow that. Regardless, Autumn knew they continued to go only because she had fallen in love with it.

As they moved into another pose and she heard another groan from the ladies, she inwardly laughed as she reflected on the time she'd convinced them to try Bikram yoga. Bikram yoga was slightly different from hot yoga because the poses were more complex and the room had to be at 105 degrees at all times. After one class, Danni and Winter hadn't been able to walk without wobbling for a few days.

"Now let's move into our cooldown."

This was her favorite part of the entire class. She did some of her best thinking during the end of class when her body was in full-relaxation mode. She wished that she'd discovered yoga when she was in high school and college. She'd heard about it, but never tried it before. Had she known she would feel so much more content after an hour of turning her body in poses she never thought possible, she would have possibly entertained a career as an instructor.

There weren't too many things in her life that made her feel normal. It wasn't that she wanted to be like everyone else, but sometimes she tired of being the oddball. The opinionated woman who didn't like weddings, who used to hide just how smart she was for fear of not being accepted. Social gatherings weren't her thing. She enjoyed talking to people, but sometimes it just felt as if people didn't enjoy talking to her. She was awkward. She knew it. She embraced it. But every now and then she wondered what it would be like to not feel more different than everybody else.

"That's all, folks. See you next week."

Just like always at the end of their hot yoga classes, she already missed the freeing feeling she exhibited for that hour. Luckily, she had enough DVDs to do yoga in the comfort of her home.

"I'm starving," Winter said as she stretched out her body. "You ladies down for some lunch?"

Autumn and Danni both nodded their head in agreement. Sunday was the only day that Bare Sophistication was closed, which meant it was the only day the three of them could have lunch together. They had a great staff, but usually one of the three of them would be in the store at all times.

They ordered sandwiches and salads at a nearby café and grabbed a table outside to enjoy the weather.

"I really am sorry about Friday night," Winter said before taking a bite of her salad.

"It's okay," Autumn replied. "Jaleen was really hospitable."

"I bet he was." Winter glanced at Danni and they shared a knowing smile.

"You both know he flirts with any woman he meets."

"That's not what our look was about, but yes, Jaleen is a flirt," Danni said with a laugh. "I still don't see how he thinks any woman would take him seriously."

"Probably because women don't make him work for it," Winter added. "Not like I made Taheim work for it."

"Girl, please," Autumn said. "You didn't make him work *that* hard."

Winter turned up an eyebrow at her statement. "I guess you're right if you're comparing it with the way that you are making Ajay work."

"I'd have to be interested to make him work for anything." She ignored Danni's giggle.

"Who are you kidding?" Winter gave her a look of disbelief. "We already know you're attracted to him, so I don't know why you'd think we'd believe that."

"Yeah, he may be attractive, but he's not my type."

"Since when is tall, dark and handsome not your type?"

"Or muscular and successful with a deep powerful voice?" Danni added. "I'm missing what's not attractive..."

"Then, why don't you date him?" she said defensively.

"Sweetie, I don't date men that my friends like or who like my friends."

"You guys are leaving out important facts."

"Like what?"

Autumn sighed before continuing. "Like the fact that we don't really get along."

"Just like Taheim and I didn't get along? Look how that turned out."

"That's different. You guys started off with that terrible blind date, otherwise, things might have been different between you initially. With Ajay, he may be attracted to me, but we don't understand each other. I'm a bit of a loner sometimes and he doesn't know the meaning of *loner*. He owns so many lounges, bars and nightclubs in Chicago that he's always around people. And I'm not a health nut, but I eat nutritious foods. Have y'all seen the menu for his venues?"

"Can you lay off the menu issue?" Danni said, shaking her head. "Seriously, you've been on his case about that since last year."

"That's not all. He has this bad-boy attitude about him."

"Bad boys were always your type."

"Maybe when I was young and naive," she said, looking to Winter. "Now I'm older. Wiser. I've dated so many different types of men and they all have the same thing in common."

"And what might that be?" Danni asked.

She began moving the lettuce around on her plate, not really wanting to answer the question. She didn't like sharing her insecurities despite the fact that the women sitting at the table knew her well enough not to judge her.

"What do they have in common?" Winter asked when she didn't respond.

"Well, for starters, they don't understand me. I'm too intimidating for a lot of men. Too opinionated for others. Too complicated for many. Too reserved for a few. And definitely too intelligent for some to find any common ground."

"Or, you've dated so many frogs that you've convinced yourself it's you, not them."

"In some cases it may be them, but the common denominator in every situation is me. And let's not forget about *him*." She didn't dare say his name out loud. It hurt too much. Made her feel *too* much.

The table went quiet for a couple of minutes until Winter spoke. "Sis, sometimes we let decisions or people from our past affect the outcome of our future. What happened when you were in high school was unfortunate, but you can't let that define your view on relationships. I don't know why you think that you won't find a man who understands you. But what I do know is if you aren't willing to give a man a chance to try, then you may never know if what you think about yourself is true."

A couple of hours later, Autumn was still thinking about her sister's words. She was usually the one giving the ladies advice, so it felt strange to be on the receiving end. She'd spent so long analyzing past relationships and wondering what went wrong. For a while, she blamed the fact that her parents' relationship was so broken she was bound to mess up. But that really wasn't fair. She adored her father, who was now back living in his home country of France. Yet she despised her mother, who was incapable of loving anyone but herself. Even so, Autumn knew deep down the problem she had when it came to the opposite sex was a result of what she'd gone through in the past.

Her first serious boyfriend had left her emotionally damaged, and even now she couldn't talk about him. Other men she dated after him had claimed to break up with her because she seemed detached. Indifferent. Impassive. Every relationship would start off going well, until things went sour and she still had no idea why.

"Or you just don't want to face the facts," she said aloud to herself after she'd arrived home. Fact: most men were interesting, until they weren't. It never failed that she eventually got bored or they got bored with her. Fact: a woman who claimed to feel butterflies when a man kissed her deeply should explain to the female population that the sparks lasted only for a short while. Eventually the sparks disappeared. Fact: a woman could go her entire life without experiencing a real orgasm as a result of sexual intercourse with a man. A fact that she wished weren't true, but understood all too well.

She went to her bathroom and turned on her shower. Her town house was only a few blocks from Bare Sophistication, and she'd fallen in love with the place when she'd visited Chicago before moving there. Before Winter had moved in with Taheim, she had stayed one block away, and Danni was still only a few blocks away.

She briefly reflected on how many women went from living independently to living with a man once they entered a serious relationship. It was understandable why that would be the next step, and she supposed men had to go through the same thing when they decided to hang up their bachelor jacket and trade it in for a nice durable family coat.

She scrolled through the music on her iPhone in search for her playlist filled with relaxing music. Once she found it, she connected her phone to the waterproof Bluetooth speaker she kept in the shower. As soon as the water rushed across her body, she immediately grabbed her plush purple loofah and dabbed it with her favorite honey-and-vanilla shower gel infused with coconut.

She was just beginning to allow the music to control her body when an incoming text message interrupted her tunes. She never responded to a message while she was in the shower or taking a bath, but as she peered closer to the screen and read the name of the person intruding on her alone time, she froze.

*Oh, goodness, what could he be texting me for?* They'd exchanged numbers last year when Taheim and Winter had gotten engaged, but not once had Ajay sent her a message. She dried one hand on the towel hanging outside her shower and unlocked her phone so she could read the text.

Hey, what are you doing?

*Hmm.* It was a little out the blue, but she was too curious as to what he really wanted not to respond.

Just relaxing. What about you?

She watched the three dots appear on her screen to indicate he was composing his text.

I'm relaxing, too. Just got done playing basketball with the guys.

*Great, now I'm imagining him all hot and sweaty.* Even as the thought entered her mind, she shook her head to try to get rid of it. She wasn't the type to swoon over a sweaty man, and she definitely wasn't going to start now.

I just finished a yoga class with the ladies.

She had barely hit Send before he responded.

Yoga, huh? A man can do a lot with that type of information.

She smiled despite herself. Ajay barely flirted with her in person, yet was flirting with her via text message.

*Maybe he's just horny.* Or maybe he was just warming her up before getting to the real reason he texted her. The water continued to hit her body, and the combination of the rhythm of the water and rereading what Ajay had written her was sparking her boldness. She wanted to entertain his flirtatiousness…just a little.

You know, they say yoga doesn't just increase your strength, balance and flexibility. It also helps your endurance…

*Not exactly flirty, but good enough.* He wasn't really flirting with her heavily, so she couldn't lay it all out there. The dots didn't appear for a short while, and she wondered if he was trying to think of a response.

Endurance. One of my favorite words. The ability to remain active for an extended period of time. What other extracurricular activities do you enjoy?

She laughed at the ridiculousness of their conversation. *Ridiculous or not, you're enjoying it.*

I also love Zumba. Any excuse to lose myself in a dance, let my thoughts float around and get a workout at the same time.

Once again, his response was quick.

So you enjoy activities that allow you to lose yourself and get lost in your thoughts?

She starting typing a general response, but decided to be more honest.

I tend to enjoy anything that lets me escape harsh realities and find solace in not overthinking everything I say or everything I do. Even in a roomful of people, I sometimes feel like the sole individual. Alone in my relaxation. Just the way I like it.

There. She did it. She'd told him something that she hadn't really told anyone before. Further making her wonder why in the world he affected her and made her want to open up. *Probably because you're secretly hoping that he will try to understand you.* But that wouldn't happen. Couldn't happen. She wouldn't let it, and she wasn't an open book. Getting her hopes up meant she was leaving room for disappointment.

She placed her phone back in a safe place away from the water. A couple of minutes later, it dinged again. *Don't read his message*, she warned herself. *You've already let him take over half your shower.* Deep down, she knew it was no point heeding her own warning. She dried one hand again and read his message.

A sea full of people and no one who understands you... I know the feeling all too well. Sometimes it's better to be alone because it gives you a chance to find yourself. To be yourself and answer any unresolved questions.

She read the message a second time, surprised that he'd related to her message and even read between the lines and interpreted things that she hadn't even written. Before she got a chance to write a response, another message popped up.

And then other times, you may be in a roomful of people and lock eyes with someone who notices you. Someone you don't have to explain anything to. Someone who sees past what you're trying to hide from others. All of a sudden it doesn't matter if thousands of people don't understand the type of person you are as long as you find one person who does... Or one person who's willing to try.

Her lips parted as she stared at the message. *Mind. Blown.* She no longer had to worry about Ajay invading her relaxing shower, because after his profound text messages, he'd just hijacked all the rest of her thoughts for the week.

# *Chapter 4*

This had been the longest week he'd had in a long time, but Ajay knew he had brought it on himself. He had no idea why he had contacted Autumn five days ago, but he had. And she'd responded.

He'd been thinking about her after his basketball game last Sunday and for some reason, he'd wanted to know how she was doing. They hadn't even exchanged a lot of texts messages that day, but the few they had had been enough to make him think about her the entire week.

Autumn was like a puzzle and he was slowly finding the pieces needed to figure her out. Not fully, but enough to understand her character and hopefully figure out why he had this insane attraction to her.

Her responses to his messages seemed to mirror

the thoughts that were floating around in his mind, which didn't make much sense. He'd been around her enough to know that they had many dissimilarities. But he guessed he must have disregarded the few parallels they might have. Before he'd known what his fingers were doing, he'd responded to her text honestly. Not that he would have lied to her. He just might not have written a message so close to how he actually felt. Up until those texts, everything had been a competition with them. He'd stared at his phone the rest of the night as their messages had continued for almost an hour after his first message.

Now he was standing outside her door debating on going inside. He glanced around the area to see if he noticed Jaleen's car parked anywhere. When he came up short, he decided to take his chances and pray that Danni was already there so that he could at least focus his attention on both of them rather than just Autumn. Inevitably, he would have to go inside, since he was meeting with Autumn, Jaleen and Danni to discuss Winter and Taheim's party.

He finally knocked on her door and waited for her to answer. When she did, he instantly felt his pants tighten just a little.

He'd seen her in dresses and jeans before, but he'd never seen her in the type of outfit she was wearing now. Thanks to having a brother in the fashion industry, he knew things that he probably wouldn't have known if it weren't for Taheim dragging him to one fashion show after another.

The coppery romper she wore accentuated her toned

legs and luscious thighs. Her hair was pulled into a high ponytail with a small hump at the top. Standing in the doorway the way that she was, there was no mistaking her beauty. But it wasn't just her looks that caught his interest. It was the confidence in her stance and the awareness reflected in her eyes. After his reaction to her, he didn't give a damn if Danni had made it to Autumn's house or not.

"Hello, Autumn. You look nice."

"So do you," she said with a smile. "Please come in."

As he walked into her town house, he couldn't help but feel as if he were picking her up for a date, rather than discussing a party. He could feel the nerves creep up his spine, and for him, that was so unlike his character.

"Hey, Ajay," Danni said as they rounded the corner to the dining room. "You're just in time. We're finally finished talking about what we want for the women-only portion of the night."

"Tell me again why the wedding party is planning this without the help of Elite Events?"

"Everyone in Chicago goes to those ladies for all their planning needs," Danni replied. "Of course they would help plan this if we asked them to, but they are already helping Winter and Taheim plan the wedding in Bora Bora, so the least we could do is plan the other events."

Ajay observed Autumn. "I'm surprised I didn't hear any grunts from you while Danni was talking."

"I'm turning over a new leaf," she said with a forced smile. "At this point, everyone knows how I feel about weddings, so there is no need to continue complaining about it. Besides, this is for my sister and the man she loves, so the least I could do is be the maid of honor she deserves."

"Look at you," he said jokingly. "After how you acted when they asked us to be maid of honor and best man, I would have never thought I'd see the day when Autumn Dupree actually seemed okay with planning a wedding event."

"I'll take that as a compliment." She glanced down and began moving around a couple of papers on the table.

"It was meant to be."

She looked up at him then and held his gaze. *I'd never want to play poker with her.* There was no doubt in his mind he would lose. Sometimes he could understand her cues, but most of the time, her thoughts were still a mystery.

"Do you want me to get the door?" Danni asked Autumn. He hadn't even heard the doorbell.

"No, I'll get it," she replied as she rushed out of the room. The gentlemanly thing to do would be to let her walk out of the room and discreetly check out her backside or not even look at all. Instead, his eyes followed her all the way out of the room.

"I don't know who's worse. You or your brother."

"What do you mean?" he asked, turning back to Danni.

She gave him a knowing look. "The way you're always staring intently at Autumn is the exact same way your brother stared at Winter in the beginning of their relationship."

"You can't compare me and Autumn to Taheim and Winter."

"Why not?"

"Because they were falling in love with each other. They had a bad first date, which made things rocky in the beginning, but in the end, they realized just how much they had in common. Autumn and I barely know each other." *Except for the things we shared with each other a few days ago.* He quickly brushed the thought aside.

"Oh, okay, I see now," Danni said. "Taheim and Winter didn't get along when they first met. You and Autumn got along great when you first met, right?"

"Right," he said without thinking. "Well, not really. She told me the food I'd ordered for a practice we had before the grand opening of Inferno Night Lounge wasn't healthy. The same way she hounded me for weeks after about the menu of my other venues."

"Gotcha. And Taheim and Winter were forced to work together for an event. But you and Autumn were never forced to work together, right?"

"Correct. We were never forced to work together."

Danni waved her arms around the room and it clicked that they were working together for their siblings' wedding. "This doesn't count. I'm happy to be a part of Taheim and Winter's wedding."

"And I'm sure Autumn is, too. But this forces you both to work together. Still, I see your point because Taheim and Winter would always steal glances at each other when they thought no one was watching. You and Autumn don't do that, either, am I right?"

He was about to respond that she was right yet again, which would validate that they were nothing like Taheim and Winter, when Autumn walked back into the room with Jaleen beside her.

He dapped fists with Jaleen as Autumn made her way to the other side of the table where Danni was standing. Jaleen started talking about something that had happened to him at work earlier in the day, but in the corner of his eye he could see Autumn adjusting her outfit. And just like that, his eyes found hers again.

Remembering what Danni had just said, he turned away from Autumn, but it was too late. Danni had caught him.

Her lips curled into a sly smile as she mouthed the word *Busted.* Okay, so maybe he wasn't being completely honest with himself. What Danni had said may be true, but they weren't like Taheim and Winter. Anyone could see that Taheim and Winter were made for each other. It may have been a while since he and Autumn had a debate, but it was only a matter of time before they had a disagreement about something. And when that happened, he'd remember why he'd told himself to stay away from her in the first place.

"Let's get down to business," Autumn said as they each took a seat at the table. "In order for us to pull off this combined bridal, bachelorette and bachelor extravaganza, we need to have a plan of action first."

"How did Winter describe the wedding theme again?" Ajay asked.

"Beach chic and sexy elegance. They also wanted a masquerade beach theme and reception. However, I was thinking that since the wedding in Bora Bora will be great, but smaller, why we don't use the masquerade beach theme for the bridal, bachelorette and bachelor event instead?"

"Can we call it something else?" Jaleen said, shaking his head. "Saying bridal, bachelorette and bachelor party every time is too much. How about we call it the triple-B party or something like that."

"For planning purposes, the four of us can call it that," Danni agreed. "But for the actual party we will need to think of an appropriate name for the invites."

"Are Winter and Taheim okay with us using that theme, since they originally wanted it for their reception in Bora Bora?" Ajay asked.

Autumn nodded her head in agreement before responding. "Winter said they are fine with it and agree that it makes more sense. For the wedding and Bora Bora festivities, we are still sticking with the beach chic and sexy elegance theme."

"Great."

"So here's the budget we're working with." Autumn pulled out her notebook with all the details she'd worked out already.

"Why, aren't you prepared," Danni said with a smile on her face. She had no doubt her friend was proud that she was finally getting involved. A part of her felt guilty for taking so long to get there.

"Now, Winter told me that they really want a venue that's in the countryside."

"Say what?" Jaleen said in surprise. "First they tell us they are tying the knot in Bora Bora, and now they want a countryside venue for the triple-B party?"

"I can confirm," Ajay responded. "Taheim said that's what they wanted. He wanted to make sure I didn't feel bad if they didn't use one of my lounges or nightclubs. But I understand that they are looking for something different than what I own."

Danni glanced at Autumn's notebook. "You would think that two city people like Winter and Taheim would want to stick with venues in the city."

"With the two of them, we should have known they would do the unexpected. Hey," Jaleen said, snapping his fingers. "What about calling the party something like Winter and Taheim Unveiled? And the tagline could be… 'A grand masquerade affair. Expect the unexpected.' Then we could follow with the date, time, and at the bottom of the invite, we could list the three Bs—bridal party, bachelorette party, bachelor party."

"That's a great idea." Autumn quickly jotted it down in her notebook.

"Yeah, I'm surprised you came up with that," Danni said sarcastically. Jaleen turned up an eyebrow.

"I'm one of the owners of a marketing and advertising firm. It's kind of what I do."

"When you're not chasing women, right?"

"Anyway," Jaleen said, ignoring Danni's last comment, "when the ladies of Elite Events planned a charity date auction last year, they didn't disclose the location until it was close to the event. It was really secretive and the PR was great. We may not want to do the same thing since this is wedding related, but it's something to think about to add mystery."

"That's a good idea, too. Since our dad will only be able to make the wedding, he insisted on paying for a large portion of this event. With the budget we already have, we're in great shape. Since we have a healthy budget, what about choosing a venue that's classic, yet mysterious, since we're going with the masquerade theme?"

"I like that," Ajay said with Jaleen and Danni nodding their heads in agreement. "I actually have a friend who owns several rustic, yet glamorous, locations, and one is about an hour or so outside the city. I could reach out to him to see if they have any availability. What date are we shooting for?"

"Well, the wedding is less than seven weeks away, so what about having the event in four weeks? Most of the people we are inviting know that we were shooting to plan something at the end of September anyway. So that would give us two and a half weeks before we leave for Bora Bora and three weeks before the wedding."

"What does the venue look like that you're calling your friend about?" Danni asked.

"I actually have photos of it in my car," Jaleen responded, although the question was directed at Ajay. Autumn and Danni shared a curious look.

Jaleen took note of the confused look on their faces. "You both know I also work for my family's business, right?"

"What does your family do?" Danni asked.

"They flip real estate, and my specialty is flipping boutique resorts. So far, I've successfully flipped about thirty properties and increased their business at least thirty-five percent. Ajay introduced me to the owner of the Woodland Creek Estate, who, in my opinion, has the best apple orchards in Illinois."

"I'm impressed," Autumn said. Just when she thought she had someone figured out, the person would surprise her. As if they had a mind of their own, her eyes drifted to Ajay's, who was luckily talking to Danni as Jaleen left for his car.

He returned with two portfolios. He flipped through one of the portfolios and gave them the other to look through. "The estate is a little over one hundred acres and the main pavilion can hold up to three hundred people and is nestled in a wooded area."

"It definitely has the feel we're looking for," Ajay said, typing something in his phone. "And I'm emailing my friend now to see if the venue is free the last Saturday in September. Might be tough with it being so close to the date, but he will have other suggestions if it is in fact booked for that day."

"Jaleen, I must agree with Autumn," Danni said, looking up from the portfolio. "This is really impressive." Instead of his normal one-liner or flirtatious comment, he offered her a genuine smile.

"Okay, so the next thing on our agenda will be discussing how we will split the night so that some of the focus is on Winter. Some on Taheim. And then, of course, combined attention on them as a couple," Autumn explained.

"Autumn and I have already been discussing what we want to do for Winter," Danni said. "We will find a way to split the room into sections. I think we all agree that this needs to be sexy, and Winter and Taheim are both designers. Let's showcase some of their nightwear designs by having models on display. Most of them are multitalented anyway, so we already have a couple dancers, gymnasts and entertainers."

"Um, exactly what type of party are we talking about?" Ajay asked as he and Jaleen shared a laugh. "Because if we're talking about inviting two hundred people and having models walk around in lingerie while dancing and whatnot, this sounds more like a strip club than a celebration."

"Not that we're complaining," Jaleen added.

Autumn shook her head at the men. "It will all be tasteful. We do masquerade events all the time, so this is a piece of cake for us. And since it is their bachelor and bachelorette party as well, the audience will expect it to be sexy. Bare Sophistication is known for bringing the sexy, so we can't disappoint. It will be classic elegance, just like my sister wants."

"Not to mention, Winter and Taheim are all about making money," Danni added. "We have to have some type of entertainment, and having clothing from their nightwear line displayed will be amazing. Like Autumn said, topping it off with masquerade masks will be a piece of cake. We got this, boys. Y'all just worry about your portion of the event."

"Oh, we're good on that. But listening to everything come together is making me think about the attire for this event. We're describing the theme in the invite, but should we explain further?"

Autumn contemplated Jaleen's words as she sent both Winter and Taheim a quick text. "Since the theme was their idea and isn't a surprise, I'm texting them to see if they want to specify attire for the guests."

Within seconds, Winter responded followed by an agreement from Taheim. When she read the words, her mouth dropped before she could catch it.

"What is it?" Danni asked.

"They chose the attire..." She texted them if they were sure and they both confirmed again. "Jaleen, you were right in saying we should expect the unexpected. Looks like our models won't be the only ones wearing lingerie and nightwear at this event."

"You're kidding me, right?" Danni asked as she took the phone out of Autumn's hand.

"I wish," she said. "They do want us to have a dress code for attendees and they want us to specify that tasteful nightwear is an option because it goes with the theme. I'm assuming we'd have to set rules, of course."

"Then, what's the big deal if it's optional?" Jaleen asked. She hadn't looked at Ajay since reading the message.

"The bridal party doesn't get a choice," she said, finally looking at Ajay. "Apparently Winter and Taheim are working on matching designs for the bridal party to wear at the event. Signature Bare Sophistication lingerie and pieces from Taheim's T. R. Night collection." Just as she'd suspected, his lips curled to the side in a smile.

"Men are so predictable," Danni said upon noticing the guys' faces. *How in the world am I going to get out of this?* A fully dressed Ajay was hard enough to avoid. But Ajay wearing sexy nightwear? She might as well just hose herself down now because her body was already on fire just from the thought.

# *Chapter 5*

"Thanks for an awesome class."

Autumn glanced over at the woman who had spoken. "You're very welcome. See you next month."

A few months ago, Autumn had decided to offer free classes to women that explained the many different types of lingerie and how one would choose the best piece for her body type. Every month they focused on a different topic and even took suggestions from the women. She had a solid twenty women who came every month, so she was really excited with the feedback.

The only problem was that they couldn't give the class until after hours when most women could make it. Usually, Danni or Winter worked the store and counter while Autumn conducted the class in one of their back rooms. But tonight, Danni had gone on a date and Winter had plans with Taheim. So she'd been left to lock up and see all the women out.

As the last woman filed out of the store, she secured the door and started turning off all the back lights. It was only 7:30 p.m., but it had already gotten rather dark outside. When she made it back to the front of the store, she began cutting off the front lights. There were still a few stores around that were open, but Autumn didn't like leaving this late alone.

"I should have made someone from the staff stay longer," she said to herself as she gathered her bags and went to lock up the front door. As she got closer to the door, she felt a chill on the back of her neck, as if someone had lightly grazed her.

She quickly turned around and stared into the darkness. There was nothing there but racks of lingerie. She looked at the dim emergency light that was at the back door. The blue color illuminated only part of the hallway. She felt another chill brush her arm.

"Please don't do this," she said to the empty room. It had been years since she'd felt this unsettled, and the feeling was all too familiar.

"It's just in your mind," she told herself. "You control your fears." Even as the words left her mouth, she felt another chill down her spine, causing her to slightly cringe at the unwelcome feeling. She supposed people never forgot their fears. You could suppress them. Pretend they didn't exist. Act as if you aren't really afraid. But did people actually eliminate their fears altogether?

Acting quickly, she locked the front door and began walking to her house. On instinct, she continued to look over her shoulder despite the fact that no one was following her. No one ever was. As much as she tried to tell herself that, looking over her shoulder helped her feel safe.

When she neared her block, the only noise she heard on the sidewalk was her heels clicking against the pavement. It briefly crossed her mind that this was exactly how women got abducted in horror flicks. Walking alone at night on a deserted street.

*I really should have driven my car today.* When she noticed her house a few feet away, she breathed out a sigh of relief and took her keys out of her bag. She felt another chill ricochet through her body as she tried to put her key in the lock.

She went to turn the key just as a loud noise pierced through the silent street, causing her to nearly jump out of her skin. Digging around for her phone, she answered the call without even checking to see who it was.

"Hello."

"Are you okay?" Danni asked. "You sound aggravated."

"I'm fine. Aren't you on a date?"

"The date was a bust, but I'm not ready to call it a night yet. Do you want to get a glass of wine with me?"

"Sure," she replied, not needing to give it another thought. "Where do you want to meet?"

"I'm in my car so I will pick you up. Are you home?"

"Yes, I'll be waiting in my foyer, so call me when you're here."

As she disconnected the call, she breathed out another sigh of relief. She really didn't want to be alone tonight.

Ten minutes later, Danni picked her up and they went to a nearby wine bar. Since one of the guys who worked there had a huge crush on Danni, they often got prime seating.

"When are you going to go out with him?"

"He's so not my type," Danni said after taking a sip of her wine.

"I know. But he's always so sweet to you." She took a sip of her red wine and relished the bitter, yet sweet, taste. "Last year, two sociologists at the University of Michigan did a study on short men versus tall men, and results showed that divorce rates were thirty-two percent lower for short men."

"And you're telling me this because..."

"If you haven't gone on a date with him because of his height, I figured you should know. Shorter men also do two more hours of housework per week than men of average or tall height."

"A whole two hours more? I guess I should jump on that, then," Danni said sarcastically.

"Just saying."

"Oh, no, look what you did." Autumn followed the direction of Danni's head nod. "Now he's coming over."

True enough, the bartender stopped by their table and asked Danni if he could bring her to the wine cellar to show her their newest inventory. He always took forever to get to his point, and she knew the only reason Danni hesitated on coming to this particular wine bar was because the guy would talk her ear off.

After a little convincing from Autumn, she eventually went, leaving Autumn alone to reflect on her thoughts. However, tonight her thoughts were conflicted. She lightly outlined the rim of her wineglass with her index finger as she stared out the front window at a couple sitting outside. She watched the woman laugh at something the man had said and place her arm playfully on his. A simple gesture that held so much meaning to someone who hadn't had a moment like that in so long. If ever…

"Is this seat taken?" At the sound of the voice, she slowly lifted her head. She had just seen him three days ago, but her heartbeat quickened just as it did every time she saw him.

"Danni won't be back for a little while, so you can sit down."

Ajay didn't sit down right away, giving her an opportunity to observe him. He had on a blue V-neck three-quarter-sleeve shirt that clung to his broad shoulders, and dark jeans that hung on his waist perfectly. Once again, she could see tattoos peeking from underneath his shirt and wished that she could get a better look. Finally, he took a seat in front of her.

"What brings you to this wine bar?" she asked. "I figured working in nightclubs and bars, you'd be tired of anything dealing with wine and spirits."

He chuckled. "You would think so. But one of the bars I own is right down the street and I decided to take a walk tonight instead of heading straight to my car. I saw you through the window."

He smelled divine. She couldn't quite place the

cologne he was wearing, but goodness, it was doing wicked things to her body.

"What were you thinking about before I interrupted your thoughts?"

She studied his eyes. "Were you watching me for a while before you spoke?"

"Yes." He didn't smirk or smile when he said it. His answer was direct. It made her heart skip a beat.

"I was looking at that couple out there." She gazed in the direction of the couple. "They don't seem to have a care in the world."

He followed the direction of her eyes before turning back to face her. "You're right, they seem to be having a good time."

"They are." She studied the behavior of the man. "Look at how his hand gently rubs her arm, but his eyes stay focused on hers."

Ajay scooted his chair to the same side as Autumn so that they were sitting side by side. Although she assumed it was so that he wouldn't have to keep turning around, it also made her senses more aware of the short distance between them. He was close. Almost too close for comfort.

"Why is the fact that he's looking in her eyes so important?"

"It's not the way he's looking into her eyes, it's that he genuinely seems interested in what she has to say. Since he cares so much about her, he cares about her perception of things. Her point of view. She's wearing a low-cut shirt. Her breasts look perfect in whatever bra she's wearing. And she's touching him as well, so you know her touch is sending alerts to the lower part of his body. He notices her shirt. I'm sure he notices her physical attributes. He can feel her touch and he's responding to it. But his eyes…his eyes only see her. A true sign that he's in love."

She wasn't sure what had gotten into her, but she couldn't stop staring at the couple.

"Is the girl in love, too?"

Autumn smirked. "She is. For him, you can see it in his eyes, but for her it's in the way she reacts to him. The way she's finding any excuse to lightly touch him. The way she's clearly excited to talk to him about whatever happened during her day. More important, you can see it in her smile." She glanced at Ajay before turning back to the couple. "Her smile is that of a woman in love. A woman can fake a laugh. Fake a cry. Even fake an orgasm. But a smile… A woman can't fake a smile. You can tell when a smile is forced. When it doesn't hold the happiness it should."

Ajay appeared to be watching the couple as intently as she was. "So when a man is truly in love, his eyes will tell it all?"

"They will." She crooked her head toward Ajay, who met her eyes. "And a woman's smile won't leave anything to question. A smile alone will let him know that she's madly and deeply in love with him."

She couldn't help but stare into his eyes. She wasn't looking for anything in particular, but it was hard not to get pulled in by his intoxicating stare. Ajay had the ability to suck her in quicker than she had a chance to process what was going on.

* * *

When she looked at him like that, he didn't know whether to push her away from him or pull her into a kiss. He'd been obsessed with her plush lips from the start, and on a night like this—when she was wearing that tinted lip gloss that he'd seen her take out of her purse on occasion—it was hard for him to keep his craving for her dormant.

Even her outfit was making it hard for him to focus. Since she was sitting down, he couldn't get the full effect of her cream skirt. However, her white blouse, unbuttoned at the top, caused the material to fall perfectly between her breasts. He was forced to adjust his pants as much as he could while sitting down.

"Did you overhear what I said that day?"

"Yes," she replied immediately.

"How do you know what I was referring to? Or what day I was referring to?"

"There is only one thing I've ever overheard that I thought you may not want me to overhear."

"And what might that be?"

She sighed as she turned back to face the couple. "That you're attracted to me, but you aren't going to act on it."

He heard disappointment reflected in her voice. "Are you saying you want me to act on it?"

"Do you want to act on it?" He expected her to turn to face him again, but she kept her head faced forward.

"It depends… If I don't act on it, things stay normal between us." *Or as normal as they could be.* "Not acting on it means there won't be any awkwardness when we attend the same events or gatherings. I don't have to worry about my brother and your sister feeling as if we can't be over at their place at the same time because we have a history. Not acting on my attraction means things stay how they should and we keep building on our platonic friendship."

"So what happens if you do act on it?"

He looked at her even though she still wasn't looking at him. "Acting on my attraction means I give in to my curiosity and I finally get a chance to experience how you taste." He leaned a little closer to her ear.

"Giving in means I get a chance to feel your body beneath my hands…the curve of your hips. The arch in your back before it expands to that luscious behind." He tried not to touch her, but he couldn't help but drag a single finger down the exposed part of her arm. As expected, she shivered beneath his touch.

"Giving in would mean I get to unleash the heat and passion that I know you keep hidden. Although I can't understand why you try to hide it."

She finally turned to him, lust reflected in her eyes. "You left out one key factor in your statement."

"Which is?"

Her eyes dropped to his lips and lingered there for a while before meeting his gaze. "You never asked me what I wanted. If I wanted you to act on your attraction or not. You didn't even ask me if I'm attracted to you, too."

Chemistry this strong couldn't be one-sided, so he sensed she was attracted to him, as well. Even so, he had to ask just to be sure. "Are you attracted to me, too?"

"A pretty obvious yes…"

When she turned forward in her seat again, he didn't miss the smile that crept across her face. He was sure this was one of those moments that he was supposed to figure out if their conversation concluded with them agreeing to act on their attraction. Or them agreeing that they shouldn't. But he couldn't seem to find the right words, and apparently, neither could she.

# *Chapter 6*

There was nothing more relaxing to Ajay than working out in his home gym. Although he lived on his own and had never allowed a woman to stay in his house for an extended period of time, his gym was his man cave. It was decked out with everything he needed, and people often asked if they could come to his house just to use his gym.

Even though he'd been working out for the past hour to try to clear his mind, he couldn't help but think about Autumn and the conversation they'd had last week. Their relationship was so different from how it was when they had first met. When Ajay thought of the people in his life he actually wanted to talk to on a daily basis, he couldn't believe that Autumn had risen so high on the list.

He recalled their conversations last year when they had initially started interacting with one another because of their siblings' relationship, but never did he imagine he'd be having these feelings now.

His phone rang, interrupting his thoughts. He sat up on the bench press before glancing at the caller ID and answering.

"Hey, Dad, how are you?"

"Hey, son, I'm doing well. Listen, I wanted to let you know that I'm taking your mom on a weekend vacation. I'm thinking we will leave tomorrow and return on Sunday."

"That's a great idea. She'll love it." His parents owned a chain of soul food restaurants in the Midwest. However, one of his dad's friends had passed away two years ago, so their newest venture was managing three steak houses that his friend had asked them to look after when his health had failed. Since one of the steak houses was in Chicago, another in Indianapolis and the third in St. Louis, his dad had spent the past year traveling between the three until he could make sure they ran as smoothly as the soul food restaurants they owned.

"I'm hoping she will, but I have a dilemma."

"What is it?"

"Friday evening, your mother was scheduled to speak to the women's support group that she talks to every other month." Ajay instantly tensed.

"Mom works with so many different organizations. Which one is she scheduled to speak to Friday?"

"The justice department's Chicago program that aids women released from prison."

*Damn, I knew that had to be the one.* "Dad, if you're asking me to speak with them, I can't."

"Son, when are you going to understand that you can't let things that happened to you in the past affect you in the present?"

"I understand that, but I don't want to participate if you're asking that I step in for Mom."

"That's exactly what I called for."

"Well, sorry, Dad, but calling me was a waste of time."

His dad sighed heavily on the phone. Ajay knew his mom was probably right there listening to their conversation.

"We won't cancel just yet. It's only Tuesday, so you still have a day or two to decide. Let me know if you change your mind."

"Okay, I will." After he hung up the phone, he knew the rest of his workout was shot. His mind was too busy thinking about the past. Decisions that had altered his life in more ways than he'd ever imagined.

His phone vibrated and dinged, indicating that he had an email. Noticing it was from his friend about the venue, he promptly read the message. Originally the September date that they'd wanted had a wedding taking place earlier that would have overlapped by a couple of hours. His friend had promised he would do everything he could to convince the couple to agree to another location since the pavilion wasn't their only choice. Luckily, the couple had seen the other space and fell in love with it even more than the pavilion.

Ajay quickly began composing a group message to

Jaleen, Autumn and Danni, stating that the venue was now available for the day they wanted. He also mentioned that the owner had agreed to let them look at the property this afternoon if they could make it.

Jaleen immediately declined since he had a prior work engagement he couldn't get out of. Autumn had originally declined, too, stating that it was her night to close the store. But Danni had quickly interjected by saying that she could close the store so that Autumn could go. He was sure that the ladies had begun texting separately because Ajay didn't get any messages for a couple of minutes before Autumn finally messaged that she would go with him to check it out.

He messaged her the time he'd pick her up from her store, then tried his best to resume his workout regimen.

A couple of hours later, Ajay had picked up Autumn and they were on the road to Woodland Creek Estate. They had already been on the road for forty-five minutes, and although they sat in a comfortable silence, Ajay was sure that Autumn could pick up on his change of mood. She was intuitive and it seemed she often picked up on things people wished she wouldn't.

"You're rather quiet today," she said as if hearing his thoughts. "Is everything okay?"

"Yeah, everything is fine. Just a lot on my mind. How was the boutique today?"

"Hmm, deflecting from my question, I see. People often do that to avoid talking about what really matters."

"Or people deflect because they are genuinely interested in learning more about that other person than talking about themselves."

He stayed facing the open road, but he could feel her eyes on him. "You know what I was thinking about all day today?" she asked.

"What?"

"I was thinking about the easiest way to reinvent the menus at your venues."

His eyes flew from the road to glare at her. "Seriously, we're still talking about this menu stuff? Why on earth is it such a big deal to you?"

"How is the health of your patrons not a big deal to you?"

"Because people come to my venues to dance, grab a beer or cocktail, catch up with friends and eat a few appetizers. They rarely come to one of my places with the notion of getting a healthy meal."

"Doesn't your family own a chain of soul food restaurants and now a few steak houses?"

"Yes, what's your point?"

"I checked out their menus online and even they offer healthy options. In the past few years, sales for numerous restaurants and lounges have increased anywhere from three and a half to ten percent on average once they incorporated more healthy options."

"Good for them."

"Did you think about the fact that you offer burger and chicken options, but no turkey burger options? You offer Southwest salad, but no fruit-and-seed salad options."

"I also offer a house salad and fruit salad. I have healthy alternatives."

"Which further proves my point that you should have a section of the menu that displays the low-calorie options. I guarantee you'll increase sales."

He was so tired of talking about this topic with Autumn. One thing he'd give her was that she was damn sure persistent. "Okay, okay. I will revisit my menu choices at the end of the year before we get the menus together for next year. Satisfied?"

"Most definitely," she said as they pulled into the estate. "Especially since the only reason I brought up your menu was to try to get your mind off whatever it is you've been thinking about this entire car ride."

He parked the car and glanced over at her. She was wearing a smile that was a mix of slyness and satisfaction. Still sexy as hell. And that long pink sundress she was wearing wasn't doing anything to discourage his thoughts about what she had on underneath the cotton material.

As they got out of the car and walked into the main building, his friend Brayden greeted them.

"Hey, Brayden," Ajay said as they dapped fists. "It's good to see you, man."

"Likewise," he said before turning his attention to Autumn. "And who might this be?"

Ajay was unprepared for the look of attraction present in Brayden's face. "Brayden, this is Autumn Dupree. She's maid of honor for Taheim and Winter's wedding. Autumn, this is my good friend Brayden Kenward."

"Nice to meet you," Brayden said, holding on to Autumn's hand a little longer than Ajay would have liked. *What is wrong with me? She's not my woman. No time to get jealous.*

"Nice to meet you, too," Autumn replied. She didn't seem to be as interested in him as he was her. But she wasn't removing her hand from his, either.

"Okay, Brayden, how about you show us the property?"

"Right." Brayden finally dropped Autumn's hand. "Autumn, Ajay shared the idea you guys had for the masquerade affair and I think the theme really fits our property. First, I'll take you both around the main house, the inn and to the apple orchards. We have twenty bedrooms in the inn, and the other party that will be there earlier that day will be staying at another nearby hotel. If you're interested, I can block all twenty rooms for your party. We can give you a very reasonable rate." Brayden clasped his hands together and started walking. "After that, I will take you down the path leading to the pavilion in the wooded area to my left. It's definitely a show-stopping venue."

Thirty minutes into the tour, Ajay realized that the venue was even more beautiful than he'd remembered. He made a mental note to tell Jaleen what a great job he had done flipping the property.

"This is so beautiful," Autumn whispered to him as they followed Brayden down a stone path through the woods.

"Brayden, are these torchlights on the sides of the path?" He didn't remember those.

"Yes, it was an idea Jaleen suggested and I'm so glad

I agreed. At night, the torchlights through the woods offer a sense of mystery and excitement that our guests love. But wait until we get to the end of the path. You won't be disappointed."

As the path opened and expanded into a massive patio decked out with modern outdoor furniture, three fire pits and an array of wildflowers surrounding the beige brick property, Ajay knew Brayden was right.

"It's breathtaking," Autumn said.

"My sentiments exactly," Ajay added. "This is definitely the type of venue that Winter and Taheim would love for their event. There is no doubt they will be blown away."

"Wait until you see inside." Brayden opened the double wood doors into a large foyer, coat closet and a long hallway with additional torchlights at the top of the wall and wooden benches adjacent to each other. When they got to the end of the hallway, they walked into the main room.

"These windows are gorgeous," Autumn replied as she immediately walked over to the floor-to-ceiling windows. When she turned her back to him, Brayden leaned closer to Ajay so that Autumn couldn't overhear.

"Y'all aren't dating, right?"

Instead of responding, Ajay slipped both hands into the pockets of his pants and shot him a stern look that wasn't hard to read.

"Is that scowl on your face your way of telling me to back off?"

"If you want to keep that face of yours clean of my fists, then yes, that's exactly what I'm saying."

"Damn, man. I'm glad that I asked before I made a move. Now that you've let me know what the deal is, I'll back off."

"Glad we have an understanding."

Brayden shook his head in disbelief. "Wow, I never thought I'd see the day when a woman had your nose wide-open."

"It's not wide-open." As the comment left his mouth, his eyes found Autumn's as she continued to observe the room. The moment was brief, but long enough for Brayden to notice.

"Man, who the hell are you kidding? You can't keep your eyes off her."

He shrugged instead of responding. No matter what he said, Brayden had already drawn his own conclusions, and if those assumptions meant he would be staying away from Autumn, that was fine with him.

There was a massive stone fireplace located in the center of the room that caught her attention next. The brick went all the way to the ceiling. Ajay had never seen anything like it. "I think it's safe to say we're definitely signing the contract before we leave today." He said the comment loud enough for Autumn to hear.

"Absolutely," Autumn replied.

"Great. I'll go work on the paperwork. There is another path just through the back doors that leads through the woods to another part of the property. I think you both will like it. How about you check it out and I'll meet you back in this room in about twenty to thirty minutes with the contract."

"Sounds good," Ajay replied, already leading Autumn through the double back doors and down the path.

# *Chapter* 7

As they exited the double back doors and began walking down the path, Autumn still seemed pleased by everything she was seeing.

"Before I forget to tell you, Danni is creating a paper invite and an e-vite. As soon as we heard this venue was available, she sent a save-the-date email blast. We will mail the paper invites tomorrow and send the e-vites tomorrow, as well. We have a little under three weeks, so we have to move fast."

"Are we disclosing the location of the event?"

"Yes, we are, since some people need to make travel plans and we don't want commuters who utilize public transportation in Chicago to assume this is a place they can get to easily. Danni will still keep most of the plans a mystery. She's only including necessary information, and we plan on working with the models this Friday so that they understand their role in the event."

"Sounds good to me." The sound of Autumn saying the word *Friday* made him think about the request from his father.

"Ajay, what's wrong? And don't tell me nothing because I can tell it's not nothing." He could hear the concern in her voice.

"You're persistent."

"Only when it comes to finding out something I want to know."

"I thought Taheim told me you were a woman of few words and only spoke when you felt as though you had something to say. That you'd never pressure anyone to talk."

She raised an eyebrow before her mouth curled into a smile. "People have described me that way my entire life and usually it's true."

"So what has changed?"

"You're not boring," she said matter-of-factly.

"Thank you, I think."

"What I mean is, usually I'm never interested enough to want to find out more about someone."

Ajay raised an eyebrow at her. She must have realized how it sounded because she immediately tried to retract her statement. She looked so cute when she was nervous and flustered.

As the path got narrower, it pushed them closer together. Autumn was looking straight ahead, yet he was looking at her. Studying her. Watching her. It had been so long since he'd confided in a woman or even felt a need to. He watched her mouth curl into a smile once again.

"It's so beautiful."

He turned his head to see what she was looking at and had to agree. It was beautiful. The stone path ended and they had to walk down a small hill that had a gravel path leading through a tall grass and flower field. Nestled in the middle of the expansive field were two large cherry blossom trees and a river that seemed to follow along the path.

Since it was so cold in Chicago most of the time, Ajay forgot how beautiful certain parts of Illinois were in the summer and fall. Even the springtime, if they were lucky enough to get a short winter season.

He followed Autumn along the path to a concrete bench on one end of the river that opened into a small pond with vibrant green lily pads. He sat down beside her and minutes passed before either of them spoke.

"Did you know that I was adopted?"

Autumn slowly turned to face him. "I had no idea that Mr. and Mrs. Reed weren't your biological parents."

"In every way that it counts, they are my parents. But we don't share the same bloodlines."

"What about Taheim and Kaya?"

"They are biologically their children."

"Were you adopted when you were a baby?"

"I wish," he said with a forced laugh. "They didn't legally adopt me until I was thirteen." He glanced at her to see if she was surprised by what he had said, but she appeared only to be listening intently.

"From the time I was seven years old, I had enjoyed

going to one of the Boys & Girls Clubs on the south side of Chicago. I grew up in an area of the south side that back in the day, we called the wild hundreds. So any excuse to have fun with other kids in the neighborhood was better than being in the streets. I knew that even at seven."

"Pretty intelligent for a seven-year-old."

"I may not be book smart like you, but I definitely have a good business sense and street smarts. Especially back then. One day, I made friends with this five-year-old kid who used to follow me around. I didn't know why this kid was so drawn to me, but I couldn't get rid of him no matter how hard I tried."

"Let me guess. Was that little boy Taheim?"

"You know it," he said with a smile as a memory of five-year-old Taheim flashed in his mind. "My parents are really active in the community and even though they didn't live in the city anymore, they gave back to the community that they grew up in. One day, Taheim had asked our dad if I could spend the night. I could tell at first he was hesitant. He asked the director of the club about my parents and I couldn't hear what the director was saying, but I'm sure he was telling him that my grandmother was my caregiver. So he walked me to my house, which was only a couple blocks away, so that he could personally ask my grandma."

"Did you used to walk to the club by yourself or did your grandmother walk you?"

"My grandma used to walk me, but then she started having health problems, so one of her friends and neighbors would take me when she could. When Dad met my grandmother, they immediately got along. My grandmother was a saint in more ways than one while my birth mother was the complete opposite. She wasn't ready to be a parent."

"I take it you don't have a good relationship with your biological parents."

"To this day, I don't know who my father is and I don't give a damn to ever find out. And my birth mom died almost ten years ago. She was in and out of jail most of my childhood and was in jail when I had met the Reeds."

"I'm sorry to hear that," Autumn said as she lightly touched his arm. "That must have been terrible."

"It was. I was conflicted because on one hand, I wanted her there. But on the other hand, her absence gave me the chance to get closer to the Reeds. As months turned into years, I was at the Reed family home more than I was at my own home. At the time, I felt as though I had the perfect life. A friend who, although younger than me, was like a brother. Parents who weren't mine, but cared about me as if I was their own. I was even at the hospital when Kaya was born, so she's only known her life with me in it." His thoughts drifted to the moment when things had changed.

Autumn scooted closer to him on the bench. "Judging from the look on your face, I'm assuming things took a turn for the worse."

"They sure did." He shook his head and let out a laugh that was filled with hurt. "My grandma passed away when I was ten years old and my world fell apart. The reason I was able to spend so much time with the

Reeds was because my grandma allowed it. When my mother got out of jail a few months before my grandmother passed, she was rarely home. She always preferred to roam the streets doing God knows what. After my grandma died, my birth mom suddenly wanted to start acting like a mother. She moved into my grandmother's house, and when the Reeds showed up a few weeks after the funeral to ask if I could come over, she told them that I wouldn't be seeing them anymore."

"That's awful."

"It really was." He watched one of the lily pads lightly spin in the pond. "A couple months later, we moved to Detroit to live with some drug dealer she was dating. The dude and I actually got along okay, but I went from learning basketball and fishing with the Reeds to learning how to roll a blunt. I would spend most of my nights in the basement with some guys who worked for him, counting the money he made."

In his peripheral vision, he could see her shaking her head. He couldn't blame her. Jaleen and a few others knew his story, but for the most part, no one knew about his past, and he liked to keep it that way.

"I witnessed things I wish I hadn't. Did things I wish I could take back."

"Everybody has regrets." She leaned her head against his shoulder, and the movement caught him by surprise. "So how in the world did you end up getting adopted by the Reeds?"

He smiled. "From ten to twelve, my life was anything but normal. The one thing my birth mother's boyfriend let me do was buy anything I wanted for the monthly party he planned for his right-hand men, their girlfriends or wives, and their kids. For me, I guess it symbolized family time. I enjoyed the parties because it was the only time that I felt normal. As if I was part of a regular family. One party they decided to have it in a public park with a nice-size pool. I was playing with the other kids in the pool but I was closest to the daughter of my mom's closest friend out there. The two of us had decided that we wanted ice cream from the truck right outside the pool area. The last person I expected to see when I got there was Taheim buying a cone."

"What are the odds? It was meant for you to see him that day."

"I had thought the same thing. I'm not much of a hugger, but that day, we'd hugged so tight and I swear, I had felt so much emotion in that moment it had been hard to breathe. I had known I missed him, but I hadn't expected to feel so much. Kids around us getting ice cream laughed, but we knew how rare it was that we would run into each other on a random Saturday in a Detroit park."

Even reminiscing about that moment almost choked him up. So long ago, yet the memory remained as if it were yesterday.

As she continued to lean her head on his shoulder, she felt him begin to relax, considering most of the time, he'd been extremely tense.

"Taheim and I talked for about an hour that day and I made my friend stay close by because I knew that as long as we both were together, my mom and her boyfriend wouldn't look for us. That was the year the Reeds opened a soul food restaurant in Detroit. It was right down the street from the park. I didn't mean to, but I told Taheim everything that day and made him promise not to tell his parents he saw me until they were back in Chicago. I had been desperate for him to understand that my birth mom's boyfriend was not the type of man to mess with. He kept his word, but my mom found out anyway. I guess my friend had told her mom about me seeing Taheim, and my mom put the pieces together. Things got bad really quickly, and not just between my mom and me, but also between her and her boyfriend. She started getting hooked on the stuff he sold and before long, he stopped trying to reason by yelling and resorted to full-blown hitting. Anytime I stepped in, I caught the wrath instead. Even knocked me unconscious a couple times."

"Oh, my goodness, I'm so sorry."

"I appreciate that. I had hoped that my mom would come to her senses and get us out of that situation, but she didn't. It hadn't mattered anyway. I was smart enough to finally call Child Protection Services. Within a month, I was removed from the house and placed in foster care. Within a year after that, the Reeds legally adopted me and as soon as I could, I took their last name."

She lifted her head from his shoulder and glanced at Ajay. "Well, I'd say that is a very happy ending, and you know how I love a happy ending," she said, trying to lighten the mood. It worked, and he let out a hearty laugh, finally releasing the remaining tension in his body.

"Yeah, we all know how much you *love* happy endings." She joined in his laughter briefly, noting that he hadn't told her how his birth mother had passed away.

"Seriously, though, I can't say that I've been through exactly what you have. But I understand having a mother who probably should have never had children in the first place."

"It's a crazy thing, isn't it? Had they not had kids, we wouldn't be here. But it's hard to shake the disappointment and hurt that you experience when you grew up with a parent who cared more about themselves than your well-being."

"Exactly. My father is a good man. And my aunt and uncle who live in Arkansas are a great example of what a loving marriage should be. My aunt and my mom may share the same blood, but they are nothing alike."

"I know what you mean. There isn't a day that goes by that I don't think about how different my life would have been if it wasn't for the Reed family."

"My mom up and left us and my dad when I was a teenager, and when she did, it was a huge relief. My dad was heartbroken when she filed for divorce. He'd spent most of their marriage trying to make her happy. But my mom is one of the most disrespectful people you could ever meet, so the day she walked out that door, it wasn't 'see you later.' It was 'good riddance.'"

"Wow, she must really be a piece of work."

"She is. Definitely a conversation for another time." She didn't really talk about her mom much because she didn't want to waste thoughts on people who didn't matter. However, after what Ajay had just shared, she knew that one day she would share something with him, as well. It wasn't that she felt she owed him her life story, but after spending her entire life never feeling inclined to share anything about herself to anyone, she finally wanted to share a piece of herself that she usually didn't. And *that* was a feeling she was enjoying a little too much.

# *Chapter 8*

"It took you long enough to get here!" Autumn went to the taxi as her sister Summer stepped out and hugged her.

"I missed you, too, sis. I can't believe I haven't seen you in months." They broke their embrace so that Summer could pay the taxi driver and get her bags.

"You know, I could have picked you up."

"I know, but I didn't want you to have to leave the store. Had I known that you would come meet me at your place anyway, I would have taken you up on your offer."

Autumn gave her another quick hug before they brought her bags into the town house. "I told Winter I would bring you by the store as soon as you arrived, so we can walk there unless you need to relax a little first."

"Nope, I'm fine. Let's go see the ladies and all the new goodies in the store that I didn't see last time."

When they arrived at the store, Summer busted through the front door.

"Never fear, sis! Your favorite bridesmaid is here."

Winter squealed so loudly, she startled one of the customers.

"Maybe we should head to the café across the street?" Autumn suggested.

"Where is Danni?" Summer asked after she embraced Winter.

"She stepped out, but should be back soon. Our sales lead is here, so I can tell her that we're going across the street, and I'll text Danni to meet us when she gets back."

"That works."

When they got to the café, they ordered specialty cappuccinos and took a seat at one of the outdoor tables.

"I'm glad it's still warm. You never know what the September weather will bring in Chicago," Summer said.

Winter nodded her head in agreement. "We've had good weather lately, so fingers crossed it continues."

"So how does it feel?"

"How does what feel?"

"How does it feel to know in less than five weeks you will be Mrs. Taheim Reed?"

Winter sighed as her eyes went all lovey-dovey. "It feels amazing. I can't wait to marry that man. And although I'm obviously so excited for the wedding, I'm also excited for the masquerade affair that they've spent so much time planning. Autumn and Ajay have been meeting a lot about the plans."

Autumn almost choked on her drink at her sister's not-so-subtle way of bringing up Ajay. "Danni and Jaleen have been key planners, as well. Not just me and Ajay."

"Hold on," Summer said, glancing from Winter to Autumn. "Did I miss something? Are you dating Ajay?"

"Hell no. We aren't dating. We just started getting along weeks ago."

"That's not what I heard," Winter mumbled before she flashed a knowing look. Autumn squinted her eyes.

"What exactly did you hear?"

"I heard, whenever you two are around each other, he can't take his eyes off you. I also heard that you look at him just as much."

"That's not true. Who told you that?"

"Way too many people to name. What's the problem?"

"Yeah, an attractive man can't take his eyes off you and you seem annoyed by it," Summer added.

They didn't understand. It was hard enough to avoid her attraction to Ajay without her sisters' input.

"The best way to stop yourself from falling for Ajay is to kiss him and see if anything is there. If there aren't any sparks, no harm, no foul."

"And if there are sparks, then you'll know one way or the other."

Autumn blinked rapidly as she looked from one of her sisters to the other. "Do you both think this type of logic will actually work on me?"

"Look, Autumn," Summer said, talking with her hands. "You may have the IQ of a genius, but, sis, you can be so dense sometimes. We know our logic doesn't make sense. But the reason we are telling you to do this is so that you can experience what it feels like to actually want someone and act on it."

"You spend way too much time overthinking your actions instead of just feeling," Winter added. "We're not telling you to date Ajay or even mess around with him. We're just telling you to kiss him and see if the sparks are there."

"Exactly, and if you happen to have sex with him, try not to think about the fact that you will have to see him at every family event that Winter and Taheim throw."

Autumn shot Summer an evil look, but she just shrugged and smiled. The ultimate little sister. Convinces you to do something, then reminds you of what you could lose by doing so.

"I don't know, guys. Logically it doesn't make sense. He's outgoing. I'm not. He enjoys being around people 24/7 while I get claustrophobic with large crowds. He's hard to read and so am I. We can't both be bad at communicating. And have you seen the women who throw themselves at him in the club? Big boobs. Big butts. Weave to their knees."

"Oh, come on," Summer said. "Those are lame comparisons. I'm sure he is not just interested in the big-booty Judy types, and even so, you have a nice ass. Besides, you're beautiful and intelligent and he'd be lucky to have you. And I'm not just saying that because you're my sister."

"Ajay is deeper than that and you know it. He wants a woman who will maintain his interest and keep him on his toes. You may be awkward at times, but from what I've heard, he seems to really get you."

She thought about the conversation she'd had with Ajay a week ago. "You're right," she said with a sigh. "There is so much more to him than I thought. I guess you never quite realize it until you truly get to know someone." Her mind drifted to how relaxed Ajay had looked after he told her about his upbringing. A slow smile spread across her face at the memory.

"Oh, wow," Winter said in surprise. "He actually told you, didn't he? I can see it in your eyes."

"Told me what?"

"About his childhood."

"You knew about it and you didn't tell me?"

"One, it wasn't my place to say. Two, all I know is that the Reeds adopted him when he was thirteen and he's their blood in all the ways that count. I also know his upbringing was hard, but that's all."

"Ajay was adopted?" Summer asked. "How did I miss that?"

"I also heard that you and he were the only ones to check out the venue last week. You both got through that without anyone getting hurt, so is it safe to say you're no longer getting on his case about stuff?"

"How about you just say that Danni told you about us—not that there is an *us*. She's the only one around Ajay and me enough. And yes, we are getting along more, so you don't have to worry about your maid of honor arguing with the best man the day of your wedding."

"Sweetie, I was more concerned with the both of you ignoring your feelings up until the wedding and the sexual tension building up so much that you can barely take it."

Summer started laughing.

"I don't see what's so funny. I'll figure out what I'm going to do about my attraction to Ajay on my own."

"Finally," Summer said, raising her hands in the air. "She admits that she's attracted to him."

"That's good," Danni said as she approached the table. "Because I just got a text message from Jaleen inviting us to his friend Luke's birthday party at Inferno Lounge tonight. Winter, he said you already knew about it."

"I did. I was waiting for you to get here before I told them. I think we all should go."

"Thursday-night party? I'm in!" Summer replied.

"Of course you show up now," Autumn said to Danni before taking another sip of her cappuccino. "Aren't you just the bearer of good news?"

"Goodness, you're grumpy!" Danni went over to hug Summer before taking the seat across from her.

"Not grumpy. Just annoyed."

"You can stay annoyed for the rest of the day," Winter said. "But tonight, you're going to Luke's birthday party with us."

"Are you annoyed because Luke was flirting with you at Jaleen's place the other day?"

"Oh, my God, Luke likes you, too?" Summer asked

enthusiastically. "I don't even know who Luke is, but Autumn having a love triangle is definitely big news."

"Danni, why do you even know that?"

"Jaleen told me," she said with a shrug. "And he had me cracking up."

"Tell us what happened."

As she listened to Danni repeat the story of that night from Jaleen's point of view, she took the time to finish her drink and block them out. If she was going to Luke's party tonight, she needed to mentally prepare herself.

"Yo, Ajay, this VIP area is dope, man. And the ladies in the club tonight are looking extra sexy. Man, this 'bout to be the best night I've ever had."

Ajay listened to a tipsy Luke rattle on about the night's festivities. He was glad he was enjoying himself, but he wished all the men in attendance weren't so taken by the women, so that he could rattle on to one of them instead.

"I'm glad you're enjoying yourself, man. I'm going to make my rounds and I'll be right back."

He searched the twenty or so people in the section for Jaleen, who was snuggled in a corner between two women. "Jay, I'll be right back. I need to make my rounds and see when Taheim is getting here."

"Bro, you know Taheim is probably in his car getting freaky with Winter."

"I'll message him." He texted his brother and Taheim responded within seconds.

"Where is he?"

"He said he's in the car talking to Winter and will be in within the next ten or fifteen minutes."

"Told you," Jaleen said with a laugh. "That dude is so sprung he can't see straight. You know they aren't coming in for at least thirty minutes."

Ajay placed his phone back into his pocket. "Yeah, you're right."

"Hey, look who's here," Jaleen said, pointing to the front door. "There go the ladies. I never met the third one. I think that's Winter and Autumn's younger sister, Summer, right?"

He barely registered what Jaleen was saying. His eyes were too focused on Autumn walking into the lounge wearing a peach dress that seemed to be made for her curvy body. Her thick hair was in curls flowing down her shoulders. As they walked closer, he noticed the strappy heels on her feet and he was able to take in her complete look. He finally made his way to her face and found her already staring at him.

"Hey, guys," Danni said as they approached. "Ajay, I know you've met Summer. But, Summer, this is Jaleen."

"It's nice to see you again, Summer," Ajay said without breaking eye contact with Autumn. He heard Summer and Jaleen exchange words, but his focus was elsewhere.

"You look beautiful," he said as his eyes drifted to the delicate earrings in her ears. Every detail about her tonight was making him lose his resolve. *You can't go there with Autumn. Too much can go wrong.* Right? Hadn't he just given himself a pep talk to keep their relationship platonic? He couldn't even remember. All he could see was her.

"Damn you look sexy." Both Autumn and Ajay, along with the rest of the group, turned to face the voice.

"Happy birthday, Luke," Autumn replied with Danni and Summer expressing similar sentiments.

"It is now that you're here." He walked over to Autumn and gave her a hug. Instead of the normal quick hug, Luke's lingered. When he brushed a kiss against Autumn's cheek, it took all Ajay's energy not to reach over and pull Luke off her. He was acutely aware of Danni, Summer and Jaleen watching his every move.

He expected Autumn to brush Luke off, but instead, she actually laughed at his lame pickup lines. She even seemed to laugh more than normal and gently touched his shoulder at whatever he whispered in her ear. *Seriously? This is how she wants to play this out?* It was one thing to politely reject someone's advances. It was another issue entirely to openly flirt when she saw him standing there.

He ignored the voice inside his head that reminded him that she wasn't his. They weren't dating, and she was allowed to flirt or talk to anyone she wanted.

"I'll be back," he said to the group before stepping off the VIP platform and walking to greet the other tables. As owner of the club, he always liked to visit the VIP guests and show his appreciation of them choosing one of his establishments for their celebration.

Forty minutes later, he'd decided to escape to the second-level platform that overlooked the first level. Winter and Taheim still hadn't walked in yet and it seemed that everyone else was having a good time on the dance floor and in the VIP section. He spotted Jaleen, Danni, Luke and Summer, but he couldn't find Autumn anywhere.

*Why are you even searching for her when you're not going to do anything?* Furthermore, why wasn't he going to do anything about their attraction? *Damn.* He couldn't remember a time when he was this indecisive about a woman. It had to be because Autumn was different. He had a feeling that she wasn't like the others because one time with her would never be enough. It would never quench his craving for her. He wasn't surprised that he'd been so honest with her last week. At the time, it had just felt right and he was glad they had talked about his past.

He started walking down the steps, prepared to try to find Autumn when he spotted her by one of the side doors. He observed her as she looked at the door and read the sign posted on it. *I hope she's not thinking about going outside this late.* He usually had a guard there, but he noticed the guard at that station was assisting with a situation at the bar. He should probably head to the bar to help as well, but he noticed the Inferno manager walk over instead.

Besides, he really needed to make sure Autumn didn't go outside. The outside area of his club was pretty safe, but he still didn't want her to step out by herself this late. He should have known that even though she didn't know he was watching her, she still wouldn't listen. She looked both ways, opened the door and slipped out.

# Chapter 9

As soon as she stepped outside, she breathed a sigh of relief. It was getting so crowded in the lounge and she was getting claustrophobic. *Either that, or I'm so sexually frustrated I can't think straight.*

She had never lusted after a man like this before. As sad as it was, she hadn't had much passion in her life, which was why the massive swarm of bees buzzing through her body was putting her on edge.

"What am I going to do about this?" she said aloud to the empty alley.

"For starters, how about you avoid walking out into dark alleys by yourself?"

Her head flew to the door she had just exited and her eyes collided with his. *No man has a right to look that sexy.* Ajay had on an all-black shirt, dark jeans and, instead of his usual style of shoes, he was sporting a classic black pair. The lines of his fade and goatee were so clean, there was no doubt that he'd just gotten a haircut earlier. He took a few steps closer to her until he was standing under the same light she was.

"Why did you come out here?"

"I needed to breathe."

He studied her eyes and it took all her energy to stand there and not fidget under his gaze. Her breathing was scattered and her heart felt as if it actually skipped a beat.

"Why were you flirting with Luke? I thought you didn't like him like that."

"I don't. But…" Her voice trailed off when she realized she had been about to tell him the truth.

"But what?"

She couldn't believe she was really contemplating telling him the truth. "He told me that the longer he hugged me, the more upset you would get."

"He said that?"

"Yes. He also told me that the minute he kissed my cheek, the vein in your neck would pop. Then he told me to see what would happen if I placed my arm on his shoulder."

He squinted his curiosity. "So you were trying to get a rise out of me to please him…or yourself?"

She swallowed the lump in her throat as her eyes bounced from his eyes to his lips. "I think it was a little bit of both. It was his birthday, so I was being polite. But I also wanted to see how you would react."

His eyes dropped to her lips. "You don't want to play games with a man like me, Autumn."

"Why not?" Her voice was so low. She wasn't even sure if he heard her until he snaked an arm around her waist and began pulling them into the corner of the building, away from lights and anyone passing by on the street.

His right hand went to her hair at the same time that he placed his other hand on the building. She had room to move, but somehow she felt captured with nothing in her line of vision but his face inches from hers.

"I thought after the talk we had last week, we'd agreed to keep our relationship platonic."

*Yeah, right! There is nothing platonic about what I'm feeling right now.* "If that was the conclusion of our conversation, then maybe I zoned out at the end because I didn't think we came to a conclusion."

"Is that your way of giving me the green light?"

It was too dark to see if his eyes had changed colors, but she was pretty sure they had. "You never answered my question. Why don't I want to play games with a man like you?"

"Because I don't play to lose. I play to win." He started massaging the back of her head. His fingers felt so good in her hair. She yearned to close her eyes. "And I don't just play to win. For example, if you give me permission to kiss you right now, I'm going to go for more than a simple kiss. I would never want you to do anything you aren't completely comfortable with or willing to try, but once I get started, I don't hold back. I'm more of an all-or-nothing type of guy."

"Is that what you want to do?" she asked when he took another step closer to her. "Do you want to kiss me?"

"Among other things," he said before his lips crashed into hers. She could hear herself moaning almost immediately, and she vaguely heard her clutch drop to the ground. His kiss was all consuming, demanding her to open her mouth and let him invade her space. She didn't have a choice. Her mind had momentarily shut down so that all she could do was focus on the way his tongue was making love with hers.

"I knew you'd taste this good," he said between kisses. His words and the fact that he'd just admitted to thinking about how she would taste lit a fire in her. She clutched one arm around his shoulder, rubbing her hand up and down his neck. He chose that moment to wrap both arms around her and brought her even closer to him. She felt the evidence of his arousal pushing against her stomach, and the feel of him made her want to rip off their clothes right there in the dark alley.

*Ripping clothes off in a dark alley?* Who was this woman and what on earth was Ajay doing to bring out this side of her? More important, what else did he plan to do? She could feel him changing their position, but she had no idea what he was doing.

"From now on, every alley that you walk past, I want you to think about this moment."

She heard his words, but she couldn't comprehend them. Nor did she like that he had stopped kissing her. Thankfully, he started placing kisses down her neck and collarbone.

Without warning, his arms went around her thighs and he lifted her in the air. She yelped out of surprise.

"What are you doing?"

"Grab the bottom of that pole connected to the staircase above you. It's locked so it shouldn't budge." She looked up and saw that she was able to reach it pretty easily. She gripped the pole before asking him another question.

"Why did you lift me?"

He looked up at her as a sly smile crept across his face. "I told you that I play to win and in doing so, that means I can no longer deny myself *exactly* what I've been craving."

She looked down at him as he lifted her up even higher. She wanted to ask him to specify how long he'd been craving her because she was so curious to find out. But she could barely think straight.

"Since I see the question in your eyes, I'll tell you that I plan on lifting you onto my shoulders and when I do, I need you to continue to grip that pole and wrap your legs around my head."

*What? I must have heard him wrong.* She was just about to say something, but he cut her off.

"You can stop me if you want, but let's not forget that I gave you fair warning. I'm not the type of guy to apologize after kissing a woman, and I'm definitely not the type of man to apologize for giving her an orgasm in a dark alley while she hangs from a stairway pole."

"Not the type to wha—" She'd had every intention of finishing her statement, but within seconds, he had pushed her completely onto his shoulders and removed her panties so fast, she barely had time to react.

"Oh, crap." She really wished she had something more poetic to say. However, she couldn't think straight with his tongue alternating between sucking her clit and dipping inside her core.

The faster he licked, the tighter her thighs got around his head. *This can't be happening*, she thought. She could count on her hand how many orgasms she'd had from sex and oral sex combined. It wasn't that she was a prude in bed, but she'd admit that she was picky. If a man couldn't hold an interesting conversation, there was no way she could connect with him sexually. *People don't just perform foreplay midair in a dark alley.* She briefly looked down at Ajay nestled between her legs, standing as if it was the most comfortable position in the world. He must have felt her adjust herself because he picked up his pace even more. *Scratch that last thought. Unless you're Ajay Reed.*

"Ajay, I don't think I can be hanging in the air like this."

He grunted and she assumed that was his way of telling her that he wasn't letting her get down. He didn't understand that she needed to get down. She couldn't handle the spasms that were already shooting through her body.

"Damn, Ajay, I really don't think I can be in the air for this..." Now her voice sounded even more breathless and panicky. "I'm on the brink and I really think I should be on solid ground."

He glanced up at her. "Do you trust me?"

She studied his face, knowing that if she said no, he would let her down. If she said yes, he would keep going. She didn't want to lie to him.

"Yes, I trust you."

"Okay, then, I need you to grip that pole. Grip my head with your thighs. And stop thinking so much. I won't let you fall and I promise you will enjoy it."

She nodded her head in agreement, and this time when he dived in between her legs, she could tell he was done holding back. She had no idea how he managed to stick two fingers inside her, hold her up and keep his mouth attached to her center. Within seconds, her body convulsed in an orgasm so powerful, she couldn't help but yell out in pleasure. Even with her thighs trembling, arms wailing and head shaking, he didn't let her go. He kept her plastered on his mouth, refusing to let her go until he was sure she felt every single bit of that orgasm.

As he finally helped Autumn to the ground, he deliberately dragged her down his body on her way down. He ignored the voice in his head that told him he was in trouble. Ajay didn't half-ass anything, so when it came to finishing what they'd started tonight, he had every intention of it.

He just knew that day wasn't going to be today. She still needed more time to process what had just happened. He was well aware of how complicated their relationship had just gotten, but he refused to regret what he did with Autumn.

Feeling her orgasm against his mouth was one of the most exhilarating things he'd ever experienced. "I couldn't help myself," he said honestly. "I'd been wanting to taste you for a while."

She gazed into his eyes before responding. "You definitely didn't hold back." Her eyes dropped down to his lips. "But you never said how long you've wanted to taste me."

She ran her fingers through her curls before adjusting her dress. *Damn, she's sexy after she has an orgasm.* Quite frankly, he'd found her sexy all the time, but tonight seeing her all satisfied and flushed made him want to see how she would look after an entire night of making love.

She looked down at his jeans, clearly recognizing they were growing tighter in his crotch area.

"I can't help it," he said with a shrug. "But to answer your question, probably around the first time we met."

Her almond-shaped eyes grew wide in surprise. "Didn't we argue the entire day we first met?"

"We sure did," he said with a laugh. "And even when I tried not to think about how you would taste, I did... Like I said, I can't help it." He really didn't think she understood what she did to him. "Autumn, I won't regret anything we do. It was easy for me to keep my attraction to a certain level when I wasn't acting on it. But now that I've tasted you, there's no way I can erase it from my memory."

He saw her shiver, but he wasn't finished yet. "I wasn't joking when I said I'm not into playing games. Mainly because I don't have the patience for it. Not when it comes to things I want." He didn't elaborate since he figured she knew what he meant.

"But I won't make a move until you give me the okay. Understood?"

She nodded her head in agreement, but Ajay couldn't read what she was thinking.

"Are you ready to walk back inside?" Once again, she nodded her head instead of voicing words.

The short walk to the back door felt like the longest walk he'd ever had to take. He felt unsettled, and he knew it was because he didn't know how she was feeling.

"Hold on, Autumn," he said, lightly tapping her arm. "You're being so quiet. I won't apologize for anything that I did because I enjoyed it way too much. But I will apologize for coming on so strong. If I'm being honest, I know I'm coming on even stronger because I've been attracted to you from the moment we met. But I'm sorry if I offended you in any way."

She studied his eyes before she let out a laugh. *What the heck is she laughing at?*

"What's so funny?"

"You are." She stepped closer to him. So close that her sweet scent filled his nostrils and caused him to stir in his pants yet again. "Ajay, you're right. I do need to comprehend everything that just happened. But the reason I'm so quiet is not because I was offended and was waiting for an apology."

She placed her hand on his chest and gave him a sweet kiss on his cheek. "The reason I'm so quiet is because it occurred to me that if you could lick me into an orgasm while hanging on a pole connected to the side of a building, I'm dying to know what you can do in other unpredictable settings. I *need* to know what else you can do."

With that, she removed her hand and walked around him toward the back door. He heard the soft thump of the door as it closed. Ajay had every intention of following her in there. He just needed to take a short walk and try to calm down his body unless he wanted to walk back into Inferno hard as a rock.

# *Chapter 10*

"You can do this. Everything will be fine. You can act normal. In the past, men have always said they couldn't read you." She squinted her eyes at her reflection, still not believing the words she was saying. *I need to work on giving myself a better pep talk.* She leaned her hands on each side of the porcelain bathroom sink and tried again.

"You excel at poker, so you've got this in the bag. No need to even worry." The loud bang on the bathroom door caused her to squeal. She swung the door open.

"What!" she said louder than she'd expected.

"Geesh, I was knocking to tell you that the rest of the bridal party arrived and Danni just called and said the models should start arriving at the pavilion any minute. Why are you talking to yourself in the bathroom?"

Autumn glared at Summer, although she knew it wasn't her fault that she was on edge. The masquerade affair was tonight and she was anxious. It wasn't that she regretted what had happened between her and Ajay in the alley on Luke's birthday, but she couldn't seem to stop her brain from overthinking their situation.

"Sis, are you okay? You've been acting strange since we got here."

Autumn had managed to avoid seeing Ajay for all the rest of the planning leading to the event. There was one meeting, which they both attended, but she had avoided eye contact most of the night and he had given her space. Yesterday, as originally planned, she, Danni and Summer had arrived at the inn at Woodland Creek Estate early. They needed to make sure the decorating crew they'd hired was getting all the details right in turning the grounds of the pavilion, as well as the inside, into a mysterious masquerade masterpiece.

"I'm okay. I can see how you would think I'm not, but I am."

"I don't believe you," Summer said, observing her. "And my guess is that it definitely has something to do with Ajay. I'm not sure what's going on, but I know you're probably overthinking whatever it is."

She nodded her head in agreement. "You're right. That's probably it. I always overthink the wrong things."

"Okay, well, I told Danni we would meet her downstairs in five minutes. Are you ready?" Autumn glanced down at her worn jeans and simple navy blue fitted shirt. Not the cutest outfit, but it would do. She started pulling her hair up into a high pony. "Yeah, I'm ready. Let's head out."

Summer was the first to make it to the door, and as soon as she did, Autumn stopped walking.

"Hey, Ajay," Summer said as she discreetly stole a glance at Autumn. "What can we do for you?"

"Danni told me we should all head to the pavilion right now, but I was hoping I could talk to Autumn for a minute."

"Um, sure," Summer said as she mouthed the word *sorry* to Autumn. "I'll see you guys soon."

When Summer shut the door behind her, leaving Autumn alone in the room with Ajay, she swore that she stopped breathing. He was wearing a plain white T-shirt and scruffy jeans secured by a brown leather belt. She could see the tattoos on his arms clearer than she ever had before, and her fingers itched to trace them and hear about the meaning behind one that she saw at the base of the sleeve of his shirt.

She'd never seen him in a fitted baseball cap before, and the level of sex appeal emanating off him was enough to light her body on fire. *It's not fair that he makes simple look so sexy.* He looked as if he hadn't even been trying. Being sexy just came naturally to him.

He walked closer to her, his light brown eyes studying her hazel ones. He looked hesitant to talk to her, and for the first time, she thought that maybe she wasn't alone in her confusion. Maybe he was just as confused as she was.

"How are you doing?" he asked, gently grazing her

cheek with his hand. The gesture caught her off guard, but instead of moving away from his hand, she found herself leaning into it.

"I'm fine."

"I don't believe you," he said as he dropped his hand back to his side. "You've been avoiding me since Luke's party. Is it because of what happened in the alley?"

She sighed and dropped her eyes from his. "It's not that I regret what happened. I just don't know how to act around you now."

"I figured that was the case, but you don't have any reason to feel strange around me. I told you that I wouldn't push you into doing anything you didn't want to do. If you don't want to go further than what happened in the alley, I respect that."

She finally glanced back at him and saw the sincerity in his eyes. "You really mean that?"

He smiled. "Yes, I really mean it. I'm not going to pretend as if it won't be hard because you already know how attracted I am to you. But besides our physical connection, I really enjoy your company and I enjoy talking to you." His face grew serious. "I told you information about me that I never disclose to people, but you made me want to open up. Sometimes holding all that stuff in isn't healthy."

She slightly twitched, understanding the truth in his words all too well.

"We'll be seeing a lot of each other, and I hope that acting on our attraction that night didn't mean that I lost your friendship. Because I really want to see where that goes, and if it turns into something more and you give me the green light, that's fine, too. But you'll control the situation and I won't push you. I know you like control, so I wanted to stop by before the entire group got together to tell you that."

Her heart melted right then. How could it not? She was the one who'd avoided him for over a week. She was the one who hadn't responded to the couple of texts he had sent. Quite frankly, she'd handled the situation all wrong, yet he was here making sure that she was okay about how everything had transpired. She couldn't even recall a man ever thinking about her feelings like that.

"I appreciate that, Ajay, but both of us were in that alley and nothing happened that I didn't want to happen. I'm sorry for avoiding you, and you're right, I'm enjoying our friendship as well, and I want to see where it goes."

"Check us out. Acting like grown-ups." He gave her a huge Chuck E. Cheese grin that had her laughing so hard, tears rolled down her cheeks. It had been a long time since she'd laughed with a man, and she was beginning to realize that with Ajay, she was experiencing a lot of firsts she never thought she would.

She was gorgeous. Intelligent. A spitfire when you pushed her. An introvert when she was uncomfortable. A debater when she was passionate about something. And as of right now, she was making it hard for him to concentrate on anything else going on at the masquerade affair.

The entire pavilion was decked out in elegant black

lace draped from the ceiling with different levels of lighting throughout the venue. Black-and-white decor with pops of red sprinkled throughout added to the chic look and the torches outside the pavilion. The outdoor decor only enhanced the classiness of the night.

It seemed that everyone in attendance was blown away by the design, and the lingerie that the attendees wore was tasteful and abided by the set of rules they'd sent out to everyone. Even though it was still the portion of the night in which men and women were split in the massive room, he had a good view of Autumn.

His parents and a few of his aunts and uncles had been in attendance earlier for cocktail hour, but as the night grew and the festivities got even sexier, they'd retired to their rooms in either the inn or a nearby hotel. Winter and Taheim had outdone themselves with the nightwear they'd designed for the bridal party. The men each had on black silk pajamas, and most of the men, himself included, had chosen to forgo the silk shirt in exchange for a white cotton tank. Each shirt had different words on the back to describe each of their personalities. Taheim had chosen Unapologetic Rebel for him, and had paired it with a black-and-white mask.

The groomsmen all loved their clothing for the night, but the bridesmaids were the ones wearing statement pieces. Each bridesmaid's piece was different. He assumed Winter had wanted to make sure the lingerie fit each woman's body type. All of the teddies or chemises that the women were wearing were tasteful, but the black satin-and-lace teddy that Autumn wore made his mouth water.

She was too far on the other side of the room for him to get the complete view, but even at a distance, he could clearly make out her delectable thighs. Each bridesmaid was also wearing a red satin robe that came to her knees, and their masks were black-and-white with a hint of red. He may be biased, but Autumn was outshining all the women in the room. As if she knew he couldn't take his eyes off her, she glanced at him and gave him a slow smile. *Damn, she's seductive without even trying.* Wasn't it just hours ago that he was telling her that he wouldn't act on his attraction until she gave him the green light? What the hell had he been thinking?

*You weren't thinking about how hard it would be to take your eyes off her.* And he wasn't the only one who noticed her. He was keeping a tally of each of his and Taheim's friends whom he saw checking her out. He wasn't going to say anything to the guys, but he was mentally preparing himself for the men he knew would hit on her tonight.

Regardless of the lust he was feeling right now, he'd meant what he'd told her. He was really starting to value her friendship, and it wasn't lost on him that he'd already opened up to her in ways he'd promised to never open up to a woman.

As if his prayers were answered, it was time to combine the room and bring out the models showcasing designs from Bare Sophistication and T. R. Night. The work crew acted fast to roll out the tables and chairs, and within minutes, Danni and Autumn gave Ajay and Jaleen the signal that the second half of the night would start. After making sure Taheim and Winter were sitting together at the front table, they all walked on stage. Autumn took the mic first.

"Ladies and gentleman, we want to thank you all for coming out tonight to Unveiled, Winter and Taheim's grand masquerade affair in which we told you all to expect the unexpected. So far, we think you can agree that this is not your average celebration." People in the audience yelled in agreement. He could tell she was a little nervous, but she sounded great.

Danni spoke next. "Now we invite you all to join us on a journey." On cue, he noticed the models and performers coming out of both double doors and standing in formation. "As most of you know, Winter and Taheim are not your everyday couple. As a lingerie designer and a fashion designer, they live in a world of satin, silk and lace."

Now it was Jaleen's turn. "In their world, beauty is in the eye of the beholder, and the right piece of clothing or lingerie can make you feel empowered. Sexy. Uninhibited."

"Welcome to a world where there are no rules when it comes to feeling sexy." The models and performers stationed around the room began moving in unison to the sultry music as Ajay spoke. "Sexy is a state of mind. A way of life. You have to embrace it." The models and performers all stopped as practiced, and as hoped, the audience seemed to be holding their breath for them to move again.

"And if you do embrace your sexy," Autumn added, "truly embrace that inner desire to unleash that feeling of empowerment and accept that we are all uniquely beautiful in our own way. You'll feel liberated. You'll feel unrestrained. Completely *unveiled*."

Another sultry song began and the models and performers spent the next hour entertaining, dancing and modeling in different sections of the room, one group at a time. Each scene appealed to a different kind of sexy, and the audience seemed completely enthralled by their performance. The waitstaff brought around heavy hors d'oeuvres and champagne throughout the entire routine.

"Check out Taheim's and Winter's faces." Ajay tapped Autumn's shoulder as the performances were coming to a close. He watched his brother gaze into Winter's eyes, satisfied that the event seemed to be exactly what they wanted.

"They are so happy," Autumn said with a smile. "Winter has already given me three hugs and told me that she never expected us to plan such a detailed event."

"Taheim expressed similar sentiments. I'm just glad that they are having such a great time. They deserve it."

"They really do. I couldn't imagine my life without Winter as my sister."

Ajay smiled as Taheim kissed Winter for the hundredth time that night. "I couldn't imagine my life without Taheim as my brother, either."

Autumn curled her arm around his and leaned her head on his shoulder. He was pretty sure she was thinking about the fact that there had been a time he wasn't sure if he would ever see Taheim again. Their moment was short-lived as they both got called away in opposite directions. He knew being the hosts of the event would mean he wouldn't have much time to pull Autumn aside, but he had really hoped he could at least share one dance with her before the night was over. As he listened to Jaleen rattle off something about one of the speakers in the room going out, he knew the chance that he would pull her away again was slim to none.

# *Chapter 11*

It was hard to believe that she was leaving for Bora Bora in one week and there was still so much left to finalize in Chicago before they all flew out for the wedding.

Leaving Bare Sophistication in the hands of their assistant manager and staff for six days was hard because the boutique meant everything to her, but she knew she had no choice since Danni and Summer were part of the wedding party, as well.

She also had a bachelorette party at Bare Sophistication in just a few days, and having to host a party before they left was increasing her stress level.

“Are you sure you’re okay with me going out with Danni and staying at her place tonight?”

Autumn glanced up from her desk in her home office at Summer, who was standing in the doorway. "Of course I'm okay with it. You and Danni have been working nonstop while Winter finalizes details for her wedding and I handle the masquerade parties and other Bare Sophistication business. You deserve a night off to relax."

"Well, I'm part owner of the boutique as well, and since I travel between New York and Miami, I'm not in the trenches like you and Winter. I owe you guys a couple years of work."

Autumn laughed and chose not to comment. She knew her sister. Summer always had something in the works. Ever since she was little, she had been trying to get her and Winter not to look at her like a little sister. They couldn't help it. Even though she was only a few years younger than them, she felt as if they'd had a huge hand in raising Summer. They hadn't been able to completely save her from the verbal wrath of their mother, but they had done the best they could.

They also knew that Summer had her mind set on opening another Bare Sophistication location. Autumn wanted to offer her some assistance, but she knew Summer would reject the help. She'd want to work out all the details before bringing the idea to her and Winter, so they'd just have to wait until she did.

"Okay, then, I'll see you tomorrow afternoon at the store. Try not to stay up too late working. Maybe take a break. Relax and watch some mindless reality show."

"Watching that crap kills brain cells."

"So you've said. But who doesn't love a good drama-filled reality show?" Summer laughed before exiting the room. After she yelled goodbye and locked the front door, Autumn reached for her glass of wine. *Maybe Summer is right...* She hadn't taken a break since the masquerade affair and she was exhausted.

She'd tried to take a breather here and there, but it seemed something always called for her attention. Usually, she liked staying busy. However, being a maid of honor was a lot of work. Luckily, her sister was so appreciative of her involvement, and because of that, she couldn't help but want to work that much harder to ensure the day was special and their company would be fine in their absence.

Her phone rang, interrupting her thoughts. When she saw who it was, a huge smile spread across her face.

"How are you, Dad?" she said as she answered the call.

"I'm good, sweetheart, how are you? You're not working too hard since you're also helping Winter with the wedding, are you?"

"No, Dad, I'm not working too hard."

"That's not what your sisters said."

"You've already talked to Summer and Winter?"

"Yes, and neither of them want you to overdo it. You and I are a lot alike, and since I know how much you dislike weddings, I'm sure now that you're on board, you feel guilty for not being enthusiastic from the beginning."

She smiled into her phone. Her dad always did know her well. He was one of those fathers who made sure his daughters knew how much he loved them. She had no doubt in her mind that he felt guilty for staying married to their mom for as long as he did, but they didn't fault him. When it came to love, sometimes it was unpredictable. *Just like whom you fall for can be unpredictable.* Her mind wandered to Ajay, as it had a lot lately.

"Autumn, did you hear what I said?"

"Sorry, Dad. What did you say?"

"I said that I want you to make sure you're taking care of yourself. With me being in France, I don't see you girls as much as I'd like."

"Dad, you do the best you can and we love that you're living your dream." After years of trying to be a Wall Street businessman to make their mom happy, their dad had decided to pursue a career as a painter. It was what he'd always wanted to do with his life, but he had needed to make money to support his family. When one of his paintings had won a prestigious award, he had informed their mom that he would eventually pursue a painting career, and she'd threatened to leave him if he did. He'd put the dream on hold and their mom had ended up leaving anyway. After a lot of convincing from his daughters, he'd finally moved back to France and pursued painting. Now he had a successful career in Europe, and she and her sisters couldn't be more proud of him.

"I just want you to give that big brain of yours a rest."

"Okay, Dad," she said with a laugh. "I'll take tonight off and relax."

"That's my girl." She talked to her father for ten more minutes before they ended the call. She stood up from her desk chair and stretched out her aching body just as the doorbell rang.

Even before she made it to the door, she had a feeling she knew who it was. Her breasts felt heavy. Her mouth was drier than before. Her heart was beating fast and her body was warm from something other than the wine she'd just had.

She checked the peephole and confirmed her suspicions. Ever since she and Ajay had decided to work on their friendship, they'd both made an effort to text or call one another. They hadn't randomly showed up at the other's home yet, but she could tell in his last message to her that he was implying it.

"Hello, Ajay," she said as she opened the door. The peephole had not done the man justice. This was her first time seeing him in lounge clothes. He was sporting dark gray jogging pants and a matching hoodie complete with some gray boots that looked similar to the beige ones he often wore. She felt a wave of awareness spread across her body and shivered at the feeling. Since the cool October night showed evidence of a rainstorm approaching, she hoped Ajay thought the chilly weather was the cause of her shiver.

"Hey, Autumn. I hope I'm not bothering you."

"You aren't. Come on in." She noticed that he was wearing a backpack and had a brown paper bag from one of her favorite grocery stores.

"Do you have plans tonight?"

"According to my family, I need to relax, so my only plans tonight are trying to do that."

He gave her a side smile that was so tempting, she almost wanted to bite her fists to keep from naughtily biting him instead. "Would you be interested in having a movie night?"

She glanced at the backpack and grocery bag, suddenly understanding the purpose of his visit. His eyes kept drifting down from her eyes, and although she could tell he was trying to be discreet, it wasn't working. She couldn't blame him. She hadn't been expecting company, so her cotton shorts and T-shirt were definitely not the type of clothing she would have chosen to wear had she known he was coming over.

"It depends on what goodies you have in that bag."

"I'm sure you'll like it." He walked into the kitchen and placed the bags on the counter. "First up, we have these nice healthy salads for dinner with dressing on the side. The salads are accompanied by a couple of chicken-salad sandwiches and roasted chickpeas. Next, for movie snacks we have white-cheddar popcorn and organic lemonade. Finally, for dessert we have chocolate coffee almond granola."

She was already smiling hard before he even pulled everything out of the bag. "You went to my favorite grocery store and bought all my favorite foods? How did you even know what they were?"

He gave her a sly smile. "One of the benefits of having a soon-to-be sister-in-law who was more than willing to divulge the information."

"Well, how can I say no to that?"

"You can't."

She studied his satisfied expression. "You really surprise me sometimes." It was the truth. She was impressed. How could she not be? He'd actually gone through the trouble of asking her sister what her favorite foods were.

His eyes darted to her lips and she licked them out of nervousness. He groaned, and although it was faint, she still heard it. "Sometimes I may surprise you. But for me, my strong connection to you still catches me off guard. So you're not just a surprise. You're a bombshell I never saw coming."

The actual definition of a bombshell could mean an overwhelming surprise or an overwhelming disappointment, and had it been any other man, she may have questioned the implication. Coming from Ajay, she knew what he meant and how he meant it. Their connection had completely shocked him. The feeling was undoubtedly mutual.

"That was a great movie," Autumn said as she stood to throw out the salad and snack containers.

"Yeah, it was great." That was a lie. Although he was sure the action movie was really good, he hadn't been able to focus on anything but how close they were sitting on the couch. He'd purposely chosen to watch an action movie with little romance so that he wouldn't feel inclined to slide Autumn across the couch and pull her in his arms. He was too damn old to sport an erection during a movie, yet here he was, still waiting for it to go down.

He'd excused himself twice to go to the bathroom and adjust himself so that she couldn't see the evidence of his arousal.

"Are you ready to watch another movie you brought with you?" she asked when she returned.

"Sure. I have a couple more options in my book bag." He stood up.

"I'll get it," she said, moving into the kitchen before he had a chance to fully stand. He watched her walk away, those short shorts riding up her creamy thighs ever so slowly. *Shit, if I keep this up, my body will never cool off.* Being around Autumn was making him test his patience in a whole new way. It had been almost half a year since he'd had sex. But the only person he wanted to make love to was the one he had told himself he would back off until she gave him a signal. Torture he wouldn't wish on any man.

He couldn't sit down any longer, so he decided to join her in the kitchen. When he found her, she had a serious look on her face.

"What's wrong?"

Her head quickly turned to his. "Nothing," she said, shoving a movie aside to look at the others. "Just wondering what we should watch."

He walked over to her and picked up the movie she'd placed on the table. "At the movie rental place, they let you pick a classic movie for every new release you rented. I figured you might like a classic horror movie."

"I don't like scary movies." Her response was extremely quick.

"No worries, we don't have to watch it. I have three other movies in there. A comedy, another action and a romance." He watched her shuffle through the movies as if she were debating between fifteen choices rather than three.

"Is everything okay?"

"Everything is fine." She continued to shuffle through the movies. Her eyes seemed distant and unfocused. Regardless of what she claimed, there was no way her mind was on the movies in her hand. He placed his hands over her fidgeting ones.

"How about I pick out the movie and you go back in the living room and relax until I get there. I'll even pour you some more wine. Okay?"

She didn't say anything, but she nodded her head and walked out of the kitchen. He'd just decided on the movie and was headed out of the kitchen when he heard footsteps going up the stairs.

"Autumn, where are you going?" he asked when he noticed her at the top of the stairs.

"I'll be back down in ten minutes."

He observed her behavior, still not convinced that nothing was wrong. "Was it the movie? Did seeing it upset you."

"I *hate Silence of the Lambs*."

He didn't miss her emphasis on the word *hate*. Instead of abiding by her wishes and letting her be on her own for ten minutes, he walked up the stairs to her. She didn't walk away or tell him not to come up. When he reached her, she sat down on the top step and he sat down beside her.

"What's wrong? You can talk to me."

Autumn sighed and looked up to the ceiling. "You

must think I'm crazy acting that way over a movie, but I really hate it."

"Why?"

"My first serious boyfriend used to love that movie. He loved all horror movies. *Love* isn't even a strong enough word for how much he loved horror movies. *Obsessed* would be more accurate."

"I can understand not liking something that an ex was obsessed with. How long did you two date?"

She leaned back on the palms of her hands, and he adjusted himself so that he was leaning part of his back against the wall.

"We dated seriously our junior year, but we hung out as friends for two years prior. I met him my freshman year of high school. School during that time wasn't the best for me. Mainly because kids never understood me. I never really fit in with a particular group of friends in high school and it wasn't until I got to college that I really began coming into my own and opening up to people. Do you remember when we were at Woodland Creek Estate near that pond and I told you that my mom is one of the most disrespectful people you could meet?"

"Yeah, I remember."

"Sonya Dupree has never cared about anyone but herself. I'm not going to get into the long, drawn-out story about her cheating on my dad or the daily arguments between them that my sisters and I used to witness as kids. At one point, I don't even think we called her mom. We called her Sonya. *Mom* was too endearing, and that woman was anything but. Winter had it the worst growing up. She saw herself in Winter and because of that, she would say things to Winter that she hoped would hurt her for life. She's learned to finally let some of it go, and Taheim has been a big help with that."

"What about you? What did she say or do to you?"

She had a faraway look in her eyes and he assumed she was thinking back to her childhood. "She definitely tried to hurt me, too. We lived in New Jersey most my life and, honestly, we couldn't wait to leave. The best times we had as kids was visiting my aunt and uncle in Arkansas whenever we could. They had six boys of their own, but they always welcomed us with open arms. I think my aunt Cynthia never understood how her sister turned out to be such a terrible mother.

"When I was a little girl, I was the ultimate nerd. Glasses too big for my face. I loved school and I loved homework even more. Several times, they told my dad I should skip a grade, but he thought it would be beneficial for me to stay with my own age group. He also didn't want Winter and me in the same grade since we're only eleven months apart. Just like she hated that Winter was so beautiful and had gotten a lot of her features, Sonya was not the type of mother who liked her kids to be smarter than her, either. For years, I tried to hide how smart I was."

"I can imagine that was hard to do. Especially for a little girl."

"It was extremely hard. I got all As without trying. I always tested at least three grades above my class. I was able to do taxes by the time I was eleven. I've always been great with numbers and Sonya never let me forget it. She'd call me four eyes. Trip me up the stairs when I had my nose in a book. Tell me that smart people would never make it in the world. My hair has always been thick and curly, and although I knew deep down she was jealous of my hair, I still believed her when one day—right before high school—she said she wanted to give me a cute style. Winter had been somewhere with my dad and Summer was young at the time. All I remember is sitting in a chair in the kitchen talking about school and twenty minutes later, she had cut off all my hair."

"You've got to be kidding. Who would do that to their daughter?"

"Sonya Dupree would. When I saw how I looked, I started crying hysterically, and the entire time I cried, she laughed so hard that when Winter and my dad got home, they couldn't hear my cries over her laugh."

"That's so cruel to do to your child. Or do to anyone for that matter."

"*Cruel* is Sonya's middle name. The name-calling and teasing I experienced from her was worse than when I was in school. A psychological bully in the rawest form. That day, I refused to let her make me cry ever again and decided that feelings and emotions were a waste of energy. The week after I made myself that promise, I ended up meeting my first boyfriend. Since I had no choice but to go to school with my hair chopped off in an ugly boy cut, I was already on edge. The kids thought I was strange. Too different for them to understand. Winter would hang out with me, but I had wanted to find my own friends."

She adjusted herself on the stairs. "I was in the school library one day and he sat down right next to me. We started talking and hit it off right away. At the time, he was the smartest person I'd ever met. Rumor around school was that the guy had some deep-rooted issues and people stayed clear of him, but to me, he had been the nicest person I'd met there. We understood each other. *Kindred spirits* is what he called it."

She grew silent and Ajay was afraid to ask her to continue. The faraway look in her eyes was gone and replaced by a look he couldn't quite define. Sad. Detached.

"Looking back, do you still think you were kindred spirits who understood each other?"

"No. Not at all. Not even a little." She glanced at him before looking back at the stairwell. He wasn't sure if he was misreading the signs or not, but in his heart, he felt as if she needed him to be prepared. Wanted him to be prepared for whatever she had to say.

Her eyes were full of angst before she voiced her next words. "Looking back, I'm angry that as smart as I am, I disregarded the signs. I hadn't fallen for my kindred spirit. Instead, I'd fallen for a boy who was later diagnosed by the state of New Jersey as a psychopath, and on that day in the library, I'd become his latest obsession."

He tried to keep his face neutral, but he hadn't been prepared for that. He hadn't been prepared at all.

# *Chapter 12*

She knew that Ajay was trying to listen to her story without overreacting to anything she was telling him, but she could see the surprise in his eyes even as he tried to keep his face neutral.

"Not what you thought I'd say, is it?"

"I won't demean your intelligence by lying, so no, it wasn't what I thought you'd say. But I do want you to continue…if you want."

She really didn't want to continue, but she felt as if she should. She never talked about her ex. It was too humiliating. Too upsetting. How many times had she wished she could turn back time to the day she had met him and look the other way? She still couldn't even say his name.

"I thought I loved him, when in reality, he'd given

me attention that I'd never gotten before. The conversations we had where I thought he understood me were just him psychoanalyzing me. Winter couldn't stand him. My dad couldn't, either. But we had too much going on at home for them to focus too much on it. He was my mistake to make."

"We all make mistakes. I told you that I did things I'm not proud of."

"I agree—we all make mistakes. I just wished I could have seen him coming. Looking back, I see all the signs now. I think about the time we ran into one of his cousins when we'd taken a drive to New York and his cousin seemed hesitant to approach us. I think about how nervous his parents always seemed around me. As if they knew something was wrong and were wondering if I'd noticed it, too. I remember a couple kids at school told me that he'd killed his family dog when he was nine, but when I asked him about it, he said it was an accident. I'd heard other strange things and had ignored them. As a matter of fact, when I told him that I heard he was cruel to animals, he'd laugh about it. I think about how any small little thing would make him fly off the handle and how I'd found dozens of pictures of me on the wall and the floor of his room one day, but he'd told me he was in the process of putting them in a collage that he wanted to give me as a gift."

"He was a friend and you were dating him, so why would you think anything of it?"

"It was overkill and I remember being freaked out at the time, but I ignored it." She took a deep breath before she spoke about the moment she finally realized something was seriously wrong.

"It wasn't until our junior year—the year we started dating—that things really started getting crazy. My bedroom was on the first floor and I was the type of person who liked feeling the breeze while I slept. I figured it was fine to sleep with the window open because my bedroom faced my backyard and we were in a relatively safe neighborhood. There were times I woke up in the middle of the night in a cold sweat and felt as if I was being watched. I'd turn to my window and no one would be there.

"Then on two occasions, we went to a park in a neighboring suburb and he'd be on a mission to only pet the dogs in the neighborhood that were brown. And it wasn't normal petting. He would always pet them slow and whisper words of sentiment to them. Most of the dog owners thought it was sweet, but I slowly began to notice how calculated he was about the strangest things. Something wasn't right.

"I finally knew I had to talk to someone when I'd noticed him writing frantically in one of the classes we had together. I made up an excuse about wanting to study for finals together and shuffled through the pages of his notebook when he'd gone to the bathroom. Nothing stood out in the notebook, except a list of names that I quickly remembered were names of six dogs we'd recently met. Later that day, Winter and I went to the park in the neighborhood and I noticed Missing posters for two of the six dogs we'd encountered."

She briefly thought about concluding the story by

ending it on a high note and tying a pretty red bow around it, but she couldn't. Had she learned a lot from the experience? Yes, she had. But after being with someone like her ex and having him be her first dose of love from the opposite sex, she was also emotionally damaged. She knew that, too. However, she was an honest person and it had been so long since she had been honest with anyone about those years that she had tried to forget. So she continued, and with any luck, at the end of the story Ajay wouldn't go running out the door.

"I didn't know what to do with the information and I figured I didn't have real proof that he had anything to do with the missing dogs. Regardless, I felt inclined to tell someone. So I told our school counselor. The counselor looked into the situation and it was later found that all six dogs that I'd seen written in his notebook were missing, not just the two I'd seen posters for. The counselor followed procedure and notified school officials and his parents. I told my dad during that time, too. The things they found in his bedroom were so eerie it made me sick to my stomach."

She closed her eyes as a chill ran through her body. "He was eventually sent to a mental institution, but not before we all learned just how sick he was. He'd documented every animal he'd ever hurt, and the worst part is, he kept something from each of them, whether it was their collar or locks of dog hair."

She finally breathed, realizing that her breathing had most likely been staggered the entire time she told her story. For the first time, she noticed that one of his hands held hers. She couldn't even recall when they had laced fingers.

"Did you ever find out more information about why he had all those photos of you?"

"I found out more than I ever cared to know. He'd removed a piece of the paneling of his closet and had books filled with pictures of me. Notes I'd written him in school. Movie ticket stubs. Any moment we'd ever shared was documented. There had also been even more photos that he'd taken when I hadn't noticed. Times when we weren't even together. Times when I was sleeping in bed…just like I'd suspected. He left me a letter, too…"

"What do you mean? He wrote you before he was institutionalized? How did he even get the chance to do that?"

"That's the funny thing," she said with a bitter laugh. "He'd placed a letter in one of my notebooks that I didn't find until months later when school had started back. I remember the last time I'd used that notebook, so I think he left it before anything happened. In the letter, he didn't express his love or anything like that. Instead, he discussed how he hoped one day I found out about the real him and accepted him for who he was. And if I didn't, he hoped I was prepared to spend the rest of my life knowing that he was always somewhere watching…looking. The letter proceeded to tell me all the reasons why I'd never be able to forget him and how *that* had been his ultimate goal all along—to make sure I never forgot. It's as if he knew eventually I would find out that he had issues. Either that, or it was a cry for help. I'm not sure and I doubt I'll ever find out."

She looked down at the goose bumps that covered her arms, but instead of feeling emotionless as she often felt after she thought about that time in her life, she felt unrestricted.

"I'm proud of you," he said after a few moments of silence. "It took a lot of bravery to go to your counselor with the information and not let that moment break you."

"I didn't feel brave. I felt scared. Helpless. The Animal Rights Society was at every hearing he had. That was all kids would talk about in school, and with Winter graduating that year, I was left to bear the embarrassment on my own with no support. I ruined so many lives that day I told the counselor my suspicions. His parents' lives. His grandparents'. *His*."

"No, you didn't. You sensed that his parents ignored the signs, and even though you blame yourself for not noticing it earlier, you can't be mad at yourself. People get sucked into the wrong crowd all the time, and in your case, you thought you'd really found a good friend. You wanted to focus on the good you saw in him, and there is nothing wrong with trying to see the good in people."

He was saying the same supportive words her dad and sisters had said to her for years, but she still felt… awkward and angry about the entire thing. "Forgiving yourself is a funny thing that I still haven't quite mastered yet."

"Don't I know it," Ajay said as he squeezed her hand

tighter. "There's more to my story than I told you about my birth mother, but I haven't even come to terms with everything myself."

"There's more to my story, too," she said with a sigh. "But I literally hate talking about this stuff."

"They say it's therapeutic, but I think we both agree we've talked about enough tonight. We should make an agreement that the door is always open if either of us wants to finish our stories."

She peered into his eyes and nervously bit her bottom lip. "So what I just told you doesn't make you want to run in the other direction?"

"No, why would it?"

"Most men would say I'm emotionally damaged and my inner demons are more than they have time to figure out."

He lightly touched her cheek. "Baby, I spent my early preteen years counting drug money for a heavy hitter in Detroit. And even though I could bring As, Bs and Cs home from school, my birth mother was more proud of me if I rolled the perfect blunt or won a schoolyard fight. I think it's safe to say that we're both emotionally damaged. And I don't even like the word *damaged. Scarred* is more like it."

She wasn't sure if her breathing had quickened because he'd called her "baby" or if it was because his touch alone always made her lose her breath.

"Since we're being honest..." For the first time, she wanted to be an open book. "Men have said I'm emotionless."

"Women have said I don't care enough."

"Men have said I'm detached in the bedroom."

"Women have said I'm good at giving, but not receiving."

"Why?"

"I don't like losing control."

She smirked. "Me, neither. Losing control means there's a possibility I could get hurt."

He began rubbing his thumb in circles on her cheek. "You lost control in the alley."

"First time ever. I never experienced a real orgasm from a man before."

He quirked an eyebrow. "So you've only experienced them by…"

"Myself. That's all. What about you?"

"Do I masturbate?"

"No, why do women feel as though you hold back?"

"I limit myself to one orgasm every time I have sex. Even if we have sex two or three times, I'm only allowing myself to orgasm once. Started doing it subconsciously years ago when women were coming from every corner when I opened my first lounge, and no woman has ever broken it."

She scrunched her forehead in surprise. "Ever? Have many tried?"

"Tried and failed."

Her eyes dropped to his lips. He had the type of bottom lip that was made for sucking. She didn't understand how she could get aroused after sharing all the information about her past, but she was. She knew he wasn't going to make a move if she didn't give him the okay.

"Would you mind if I try to break your orgasm limit?"

"Only if you don't mind me convincing you that those men who told you that you're emotionless and detached in the bedroom didn't deserve you anyway."

"I'd like that."

"Then, you have yourself a deal."

They sat on the steps a little while longer before Ajay suggested they watch the comedy he brought. When they got to the end of the steps, he swung her around and planted a sweet kiss on her lips before bringing her in for a hug. She had never been much of a hugger, but standing there, hugging Ajay, she felt as if she didn't have a care in the world.

"It's so beautiful," Danni said quietly as she dabbed the corners of her eyes.

"Such an adorable scene," Summer added.

"This couple had the right idea," Autumn whispered. "Saving loads on costs."

Ajay stole a glance at Jaleen, who looked about as enthusiastic as he felt. Although Danni, Summer and Autumn had been on the same flight, and he and Jaleen had been on the same flight, the five of them had arrived in Bora Bora around the same time and agreed to meet up and take the same boat to their luxury resort.

"Ladies, the boat leaves in ten minutes. Maybe we should make our way there," Ajay suggested.

"Just one more minute," Danni replied.

Ajay looked at Jaleen and shrugged before resuming to witness the couple who had chosen to get married right outside the French Polynesia International Airport. It was unlike anything he'd ever seen. They were speaking another language so he couldn't understand the words they voiced when they exchanged vows. It didn't seem to matter to the women, because they were completely enthralled by the sight. It was also hard to enjoy the ceremony when the men were the ones holding all the bags.

"Okay, now it's time to go," Jaleen said as the couple shared a passionate kiss. They made their way to the boat and boarded with a host of other vacationers.

He'd known that Bora Bora would be beautiful, but he'd had no idea just how much. When the plane had initially approached their destination, he'd been immediately taken by the mountains covered in luscious greenery. It was the type of scenery one often dreamed of when thinking of paradise.

Ajay heard Jaleen laugh and turned to see what had caught his friend's interest. As usual, it had to do with women.

"You know what I just found out?" Jaleen asked, linking an arm over Ajay's shoulder.

"What?"

"Those ladies over there told me that Bora Bora is where they filmed *Couples Retreat*. Did you know that?"

"I didn't," Ajay said with a laugh. "But I have to admit, that actually is interesting."

"That's what I was telling the ladies," Jaleen said loud enough for them to hear. "And we need to find that singles island that they showed in that movie." When

Jaleen walked back over to them, they giggled and were clearly enjoying the flirting. Ajay glanced at Danni, Summer and Autumn in time to see each of them roll their eyes.

As he walked over to the railing and admired the rich South Pacific scenery, he vaguely overheard Jaleen mention his name to the women. He hoped he wasn't implying that he was his wingman or that he was single. That may be the case, but in his heart, he wasn't up for grabs.

Last week at movie night at Autumn's home, it had gone much better than expected. Listening to her describe what she'd gone through with her ex had been harder than he'd ever imagined. The experience had impacted her deeply, and even though he was a firm believer in certain things happening for a reason, it was a lesson he wished she could have avoided. The rest of the night had gone smoothly. She'd curled herself into his arms as they'd watched a comedy, and by the end of the movie, they had both fallen asleep on the couch. He hadn't awakened until the morning when he felt her stir in his arms.

With any other woman, the situation may have been awkward for him, but with Autumn, it had felt right. Perfect. They just fit.

"Care for company?" Autumn said as she slid beside him.

"Your company? Always." He meant the words more than she probably realized.

"I'm not sure if I thanked you for listening to my story the other day..."

He cut her off midsentence. "You'll never have to thank me for listening to you. I wanted to know your story and I appreciate you trusting me enough to tell me about your past."

"Most of the men I've come across haven't felt that way."

"Good thing I'm not most men." His eyes captured hers, daring her to deny what he was saying. He needed her to understand how he felt. He wanted her to know that even though the ball was in her court, he wasn't going to stop trying to get to know her. Friendship. Relationship. He didn't put too much thought into one versus the other because all he knew was that he wanted her—all of her—in any capacity.

She looked away first and stared out into the ocean, but he kept his eyes trained on her. He'd never been the jealous type, but he wouldn't spend the next six days in Bora Bora watching the other groomsmen flirt with her and pretend as if she wasn't the main thing on his mind. The *only* thing on his mind.

# *Chapter 13*

"This place is absolutely breathtaking," Autumn said as she entered the overwater bungalow that she'd be residing in for the next six days. The pictures she'd seen online had been beautiful, but not nearly as stunning as experiencing the resort firsthand.

The stilted thatch-roofed villas of the resort were nestled around a crystal clear turquoise lagoon. She hadn't been around the entire resort grounds yet, but from the minute they'd exited the boat, she'd been impressed with the attentive staff.

She walked into the living room area that was complete with beige wicker furniture, plush white cushions and decorative pillows. Slipping off her sandals, she wiggled her toes against the cool exotic wood showcased throughout the entire space. Pockets of glass-paneled floors offered an amazing view of the fish and plant life in the lagoon. The bathroom was complete with marble double sinks, a standing waterfall shower and grand cast-iron tub.

As she turned the corner to the bedroom, a large king canopy bed came into view with clean white sheets and vibrant pillows that matched the ones in the living room. Her eyes wandered to the open glass doors that led to a wraparound deck. Stepping outside, the sun kissed her skin and reflected off the water. The outdoor plunge pool looked so enticing, she almost slipped off her sundress so that she could cool off.

She walked to the edge of the deck and peeked over at the stepladder that was there so guests were only steps away from a dip in the lagoon.

"Pretty amazing, isn't it?"

She turned to the side at the sound of Ajay's voice. "Are you staying in that villa?" She had been the first person to be shown her room, so she wasn't sure if maybe he was just checking out Summer's, Danni's or Jaleen's villa, or if it was his.

"It's Jaleen's."

"Oh," she said, trying to hide her disappointment. "Okay."

"Did you want it to be mine?"

She sighed as she glanced at him across their decks. At this point, she was pretty sure he knew how much she enjoyed his company. "What do you think?"

"I think you wanted our villas to be next to one another." His lips curled into a smile. "Which is why I'm glad this is indeed where I will be staying. Even if it hadn't been, I would have made someone switch with me."

"If that's how you want to start this trip, you should prepare for retaliation."

"I have a feeling I'd like the way you retaliate." Even from a distance, her body warmed under his gaze. She was already intrigued by her attraction to him, but after the way he'd comforted her when she'd told him the story about her ex, she hadn't been able to think about anything but the bet they'd made. The agreement that he could work on changing the way she viewed herself in relationships while she would try to get him to lose control during intimacy. It wasn't lost on her that by making that agreement, there was no way they wouldn't be taking their relationship to the next level.

"We should probably get ready to meet the others," she suggested. The bridal party had promised they would meet with Winter and Tahcim as soon as they had all arrived so that they could discuss the plans for the week leading up to the wedding.

It was their first night in Bora Bora, and already the day had been busy with planning. Guests would be sprinkling in over the next few days, and the only rule that Taheim and Winter had for the bridal party was that she wanted them all there early. Of course, since a couple of the groomsmen and bridesmaids were married, their significant others had already arrived, so the welcome beach bonfire was in full swing.

"Seriously, can you stop staring at her for one minute?"

Ajay cut his eyes at Jaleen. "Aw, Jay, I didn't know you needed my undivided attention."

"He doesn't get it, Ajay, but I think one day some woman is going to make him want to turn in his player card." The comment came from Jaleen's friend and business partner Daman Barker, who was also a groomsman and married to Elite Events cofounder Imani Rayne-Barker. All four founders of Elite Events Inc. were present since Imani and her sister, Cydney Rayne-Miles, were the lead planners for the wedding and were working closely with the resort's event planner. The other two cofounders, Mya Winters-Madden and Lex Turner-Madden, were bridesmaids and married to Winter's cousins Malik and Micah Madden.

"Ha! Y'all are some fools if you think I'm going to let some chick get my nose wide-open. There isn't a woman in the world who could tame me."

Ajay and Daman shared a knowing look.

"You both can look at each other all you want. I know myself better than y'all do. Just because everybody in Chicago seems to want to get married lately, that doesn't mean I'm suddenly going to change my mind. I'm happy for each of you, but I'll keep my player card, thank you."

"You say that now. Then suddenly you meet a woman who makes you think about things you never used to think about."

"Ajay, man, I already know how you feel about Autumn. That's why I played matchmaker with you two. But I'm not the type of man a woman settles down with."

"You're damn right," Danni said as she approached the men. "And any woman who is able to finally break you of your bad habits will have a helluva lot of work to do."

"Who said my habits are bad?"

Danni perched one arm on her hip. "Why did one of those women you were flirting with on the boat curse you out when we were at the bar?"

"How am I supposed to know? I was just as confused as you were."

"Oh, I wasn't confused. She claimed you had just been in her villa and then she saw you flirting with one of the resort staff members."

"She's nuts if she thought I would only talk to her on this vacation, so that's her fault. I never implied otherwise."

"We can talk about your doggish ways later. I actually came over because Imani was looking for Daman."

"Is she okay?"

"She's fine. Just feeling a little under the weather."

Ajay wondered if that was code for saying she was pregnant with their second child. They hadn't made an announcement, but in addition to engagements happening all over the place, babies were being born.

A feminine laugh caught his ear toward the other side of the bonfire. He turned in time to see Luke approach Autumn.

*Man, this dude won't quit.* Even though on his birthday, Luke told Autumn he was just flirting to make him jealous, he didn't believe for one second that Luke had walked over to her for the same reason.

"Your assumptions are right, you know," Jaleen said.

Ajay took a sip of his drink. "About what?"

"About Luke trying to hit on your woman."

"She's not my woman."

"Men are so complicated," Danni said, shaking her head.

"All I'm saying is that Luke and I were talking earlier and he was talking about how sexy Autumn looked and how a little friendly competition between men didn't hurt."

"This dude clearly doesn't know me. And he's not competition. To compete with me, we have to be on the same level, and she's not interested in him."

"How can you be so sure?" Danni asked.

"Look at her body language," he said, nodding his head toward Autumn and Luke. "She's bored by whatever it is that he's saying to her. You can tell her smile isn't genuine, it's forced." Ajay observed them a little more closely. "He doesn't even care about what she's saying. He's looking everywhere but in her eyes. He's not connecting with her and she looks as if she wants to excuse herself, but she's trying not to be rude."

As if she'd heard what he said, Autumn excused herself from the group and walked toward the dimly lit path leading to the bar.

"Wow," Jaleen said. "I'm impressed."

Ajay didn't even hear the rest of whatever it was that Jaleen and Danni were saying to him. He was too focused on following Autumn, and he wasn't the only one. Luke was coming from the other side of the beach.

When he was a couple of feet away, Ajay quickened his pace and caught Autumn by the waist.

"What the—" Her words were momentarily hushed when he placed his hand over her mouth and pulled them both into the lush trees. Moments later, Luke glanced around the path, obviously trying to figure out where they were.

Her eyes twinkled in amusement as she pieced together why he'd pulled her off the path. He slowly removed his hand from her mouth as they both waited for Luke to leave. After a few more seconds, he finally went back to the beach and they were able to release the laughs they were both holding in.

"You were watching Luke and me at the bonfire?"

"You mean watching Luke attempt to flirt with you? Yeah, I was watching."

"Attempt?" she asked, adjusting her back on the tree that she was leaning on. "How can you be so sure that he didn't succeed in his flirtation?"

"Come on, you know me better than that." He brushed a couple of strands of hair out of her face. "Your body language was indifferent, yet friendly. You didn't want him to feel bad, so you smiled. But your smile was forced. Don't get me wrong, he's definitely attracted to you. But he doesn't see *you*." He pointed to her heart. "Wanting to get you into bed and wanting to actually get to know the real you are not the same thing."

She fidgeted, causing her thigh to brush against his crotch. "Am I to assume you don't want to get in my bed?"

"I'm not going to answer that."

"Why not?"

He placed his hands on each side of the tree. His gaze fixated on her lips. "You already know I want to get you in my bed. And I'm confident that you also know I want to get to know you as much as I can, too."

"I know," she said, dipping out her tongue to moisten her lips. "I want that, too." When her tongue dipped out of her mouth for a second time, he couldn't resist tasting her again.

She lifted her head at the same time that he dropped his and seized her sweet honey lips. *This is what I've been waiting for.* He was slowly learning that any time not spent kissing Autumn Dupree was a waste of time. When he wasn't kissing her, he was thinking about kissing her...dreaming about kissing her. It was crazy how much she occupied his thoughts. How much he was enthralled with her mind, not just her body.

When her arms wrapped around his neck, he felt her leg located closest to his crotch begin to lift. He removed one hand from the tree to grasp her thigh and hold her steady. Her thigh was hot to the touch, and feeling her milky skin in his hands only made him increase the kiss.

*A woman this soft should never be allowed to wear clothes.* He didn't want anything damaging her delicate skin, so he switched their positions so that his back was to the tree instead. She nestled her delicious body in the cove of his legs, neither of them breaking their kiss.

Their kiss slowed when he heard the sound of drums

beating in the close distance, which signaled that the Polynesian dance was about to begin.

"Our families will kill us if we aren't present to watch the dance. I think we have to give the welcome speech right after," she said between kisses.

"Taheim will understand." He dragged his lips from hers to place kisses along her neck and collarbone.

"Winter won't understand."

"You're going to have to say something more convincing to get me to stop kissing you right now, because I don't give a damn if they get mad at us."

"Something told me you wouldn't care." She eased her head away from him and attempted to step out of his arms. "Ajay, I don't want to stop, either, but we really need to get back. We have five more days left in paradise, and that's plenty of time for us to pick this up at another appropriate time."

Deep down, he knew she was right. But damned if he cared. "Okay, then, you have to leave out first."

"Can't we just go to the bar and get drinks before returning? People will just assume we were there the entire time."

He looked down at the bulge in his pants. "No can do, sweetheart. I need you about twenty feet away from me if you want me to return to that bonfire." She peeked down at his pants before lifting her head back to his with a big smile on her face.

"There is nothing funny about me returning to that party with a bulge in my pants. It seems every make-out session with you leads to embarrassment for me. A grown-ass man looking like a horny-ass teenager."

She let her body fall back into his arms. "Maybe just a couple more minutes," she said as she slowly brought her lips back to his.

*I could get used to this*, he thought as his tongue continued to meet hers stroke for stroke.

# *Chapter 14*

The sun had just begun to set over the stunning Mount Otemanu and Autumn had been doing yoga in a reclusive part of the resort for the past thirty minutes. She really had no choice. Her body needed to focus on something other than how sexually frustrated she was.

After making out with Ajay for at least fifteen minutes last night, they had finally returned to the bonfire in time to catch the end of the performance and give their short welcome speeches. She'd had every intention of returning to her villa and giving Ajay an invitation to join her, but had gotten sidetracked by the surprise—Winter and Taheim had planned to take the group to a neighboring resort for a reggae concert that was going on.

The concert was great and everyone had enjoyed

themselves. However, after the concert, the women and men separated. The women had found themselves in Summer's villa talking and drinking the night away. She had no idea where the guys had ended up.

The entire time she was with the women, she'd been checking her watch to see the minutes tick away, along with her chance to invite Ajay to her room. By the time morning rolled around, they were off to do another group activity, ruining any intention she had of presenting him with her idea in the morning. Clearly, Winter and Taheim were going to have them too busy to even think about getting freaky in paradise. So now she found herself attempting to use the remaining sunlight to relieve the tension in her body before they met the group for dinner.

After twenty more minutes of yoga, she felt better than she had since she'd arrived to Bora Bora. She was just making her way back to the path leading to the villas when she noticed a man running in the distance toward her direction wearing a white T-shirt and basketball shorts. She stepped back into the space she'd just vacated to wait for him to pass.

As the man got nearer, she stepped back even farther out of view. She knew that body. That swag. Even though she'd never seen him run before. Even if she hadn't recognized him, her lady parts were coming to life, indicating that there was no doubt Ajay Reed was the man jogging down the path.

His phone was in a sleeve tied to his arm, and even though she couldn't see headphones in his ear, she was sure he was listening to music. She found herself holding her breath as he approached, praying he didn't see her. She didn't really know why she didn't want him to see her, it was just that she preferred to view him from a distance.

She glanced down at her stretch capris and tank top and subconsciously brushed her hands over curlicues that had escaped her ponytail. *Definitely not cute enough to run into him.* Mind made up, she stayed hidden and waited for him to pass her, closing her eyes when he was close enough to spot her. She didn't open her eyes until she heard his footsteps pass. When he was out of sight, she finally got on the path and started walking in the direction of the villas.

*I wonder where he was going...* She didn't know he was a runner, but that made sense. He had the body of a runner. Or a football player. Either way, running suited him and he looked damn good doing it.

*Why did you close your eyes when he passed by you?* That had been a stupid move. She'd admired him from a distance, but closed her eyes out of nervousness when he had gotten close enough for her to really see him.

*I should catch up with him.* She wasn't much of a runner, but she was athletic enough to catch up with him if she ran at a fast pace. Besides, she was in paradise and that meant she wasn't backing down to whatever Bora Bora had in store.

She turned around, clutched her purple-and-black yoga mat under her arm and started running in the direction that Ajay had gone. Within minutes, he came into view again. She yelled his name a couple of times and didn't get a response.

"He must have his headphones in," she said to herself. She was about to give up when he stopped running but continued to jog in place. She started running again, confident that she could catch up with him this time. He glanced to his left and pushed a few plants aside. Next thing she knew, he was making his way through the plants.

"What the hell is he doing?" She caught up to the spot where he'd been standing and looked through the plants he'd just pushed aside, and kept pushing until she reached a clearing near a host of large trees. Glancing to her right and left, she wondered which way he went.

*This is nuts*, she thought. *Why the heck am I following him?* Even though she questioned her actions, now her curiosity was getting the best of her. She walked a few feet to the left and through another row of tall plants, and she spotted him standing near the water, removing his earbuds and phone holder before placing it on the ground.

She took two steps forward with every intention of making her presence known when he started removing his shirt. For the second time in ten minutes, her breath caught in her throat.

She'd never seen him bare chested before, and even with his back to her, she could tell he was a sight to see. His back and broad shoulders were so defined and structured. As if a sculptor had taken a piece of rock and chiseled the hard material into his delectable body. She could see more of his tattoos than before, but couldn't make out what they were.

He stretched his body to the left, then the right before he lifted alternating knees a few times and twisted his body. She became engrossed by his muscular biceps and powerful-looking calves. She already knew he had tattoos on his arms, but knowing that didn't stop her from salivating.

His hands went to the waistband of his gym shorts and boxers. *Oh, my word, what am I going to do if he takes them off?* She felt as if she was a teenager who wasn't old enough to get into a rated-R movie, but had sneaked in anyway. Without noticing what she was doing, she leaned closer, as if leaning closer would allow her to see something she couldn't quite see.

A plant that she'd been holding back before she leaned closer popped directly in front of her, blocking her vision. She didn't want to miss the show, so she moved it without thinking about the yoga mat that was tucked under her arm. It dropped with a slight thump, causing Ajay to turn around. She dropped to the ground, praying that he didn't see her. She could tell by the position of his feet he was still facing her direction. After a few more seconds, she finally saw his feet turn back toward the water.

*Thank goodness. That would have been so embarrassing.* A part of her was embarrassed anyway. She'd never spied on a man before, much less chased him through plants and trees. Just as she crouched and picked up her yoga mat, preparing to vacate the area, his head tilted to the side in a slight smile and he dropped his shorts and boxers.

"Oh, shit," she whispered, mesmerized by the work of art standing before her. She didn't curse a lot, but there was no other way to voice the way she felt upon seeing all six-foot-two of Ajay Reed. His ass alone was the kind that made women clench their thighs together and imagine what it would be like to squeeze it…bite it…slap it.

He stretched again and Autumn moaned at the way the sun setting in the distance cast a soft glow over his phenomenal body. *With a physique like that, who needs to wear clothes?* And Ajay was the type to wear three-quarter-sleeve shirts and jeans in the summer even though it was hot as hell outside. She made a mental note to contemplate sneaking into his villa and hiding all his clothes.

He finally stopped stretching and went into the water. When his head dipped under, she made a mad dash out of the plants, through the trees and to the path. By the time she made it to her villa, it had officially gotten dark and she realized her clothes were filthy from lying in the dirt when she was spying on Ajay. As she began taking off her clothes to take a shower and get ready before dinner, she imagined that he was there taking her clothes off instead.

She should regret what she'd done. She should feel bad for spying on him. She should confess and pretend as if she hadn't seen him get naked before getting into the water. But she wasn't sorry. Not one bit. And there was no way she was disregarding what she'd seen. If anything, it would be etched in her memory forever.

*I would love to see this view every day*, Ajay thought as he sat on his deck and listened to the calming sounds of nature. He was running late for dinner, but he didn't care. He needed a moment to himself. Ever since he'd arrived to Bora Bora, he had been doing a lot of self-reflection, and in doing so, he'd realized that his parents were right. He had to come to terms with his past.

Talking about it and not letting it define him was one thing, but he still had a few issues to work through. He'd always known that he wouldn't get over his past overnight, but being in a place that was closer to paradise than he had ever been was good for the soul. Good for the mind. His phone rang, interrupting his thoughts.

"What's up, Jaleen?"

"What's taking you so long to get here?"

"Don't get your panties in a twist. I'm coming."

"Good, because your parents just got here, too."

"Okay, I'm leaving my villa soon." He went back inside and placed his leather wallet into the pocket of his slacks.

"I'll let Danni and Summer know. They were hounding me about you two."

"Two? I'm by myself."

"Well, Autumn isn't here, either, so we assumed you two were together. Since you're neighbors, can you knock on her door and see what's taking her so long?"

"Sure." He hung up and took the short walk over to Autumn's villa. He knocked and there was no answer, so he tried a second time. By the third knock, she answered.

"Sorry, I fell asleep after I got out of the shower. I only woke up because I heard you knocking."

Her mouth was still moving, but he barely comprehended her words. He was too mesmerized by the sight of her in a thin piece of white fabric that was clinging to all her soft curves. Her hair draped over her shoulders in tendrils of curls, evidence that she'd washed it.

"Can you wait for ten minutes while I get dressed quickly?" She moved aside so he could enter the villa. He barely recalled shutting the door. He was already following her to her suitcase located in the bedroom.

"I have several missed calls from the girls. Did they send you to get me?"

She'd asked him a question. He'd heard it, and by the look on her face, she expected him to answer it.

"No." There, he'd answered. She looked at him inquisitively, oblivious to the inner struggle he was having. He could see the outline of her nipples through the material and wondered if she was wearing any panties since she wasn't wearing a bra. The fact that he didn't know for sure was driving him crazy.

"I should probably wear a dress." She walked over to the closet and began shuffling through hanging dresses. Every time she moved, his eyes zoned in on the natural jiggle of her round, spankable butt. Then she had the nerve to slightly bend over and look through her shoes before returning to the dresses.

She was still talking, and he was pretty sure she was still asking him questions, but he couldn't stay focused. He'd only just noticed her phone was docked on a speaker and slow music was filling the room. "Are you doing this on purpose?" he asked, finally finding his voice. Her hands stopped moving and she peered at him over her shoulder.

"Not at first," she said, turning around to face him. "I hadn't thought about my lack of clothing until you stopped talking and just stared at me. So I figured I could get embarrassed or do something about it."

He swallowed hard. "Seeing you when you opened the door rendered me speechless."

"You finally found your voice."

"Barely." His voice had gone from deep to downright husky. The catch in her breath proved she had heard it, too. He was done dancing around their limitless attraction. Done holding back on something he knew was meant to happen.

He walked over to her. Slow…purposeful. With each step he took, he kept his eyes concentrated on her, enjoying the way her chest heaved in and out the closer he got. From the start, timing had been everything for them, but right now he didn't give a damn about anything but her.

When he reached her, he dropped his forehead to hers and closed his eyes, relishing the way her clean scent filled his nostrils. He didn't want to rush this. He needed to savor her. Cherish her. She meant too much for him to rush. He lifted his forehead and gazed into her eyes. Her hazel eyes sparkled with light brown and gold flecks, potent arousal evident in the way she stared back at him.

Her hands rose to his shirt, and she unbuttoned it slowly. Every finger that grazed his chest left a hot trail where she'd just touched. She eased the shirt off his shoulders and let it drop to the floor. Next, her hands went to the belt of his slacks. He kicked them to the side to join his shirt.

She trailed a finger down his stomach before rolling her tongue over the crevices of his abs. Her tongue was hot and the moisture was causing him to become even more aroused. He couldn't wait anymore. He had to see her.

His hands reached the bottom of her nightie, and slowly he pulled the material up her body. Within seconds, he'd confirmed his suspicions. She wasn't wearing any panties, and the thin patch of hair leading to the object of his desire was so beautiful, his mouth dried.

By the time he pulled the fabric over her perfect breasts, he was sure he was already drooling. He yanked the rest off her body and tossed the nightie to join his discarded clothes. He wasn't sure what to expect when he had her naked, but he'd hoped that she wouldn't get nervous and try to cover herself. He was relieved when instead of being bashful, she let him have his fill. He watched the goose bumps rise on every part of her body that his eyes landed on. The fact that he could make her shiver just by looking at her made it even more impossible to take things slow.

Without warning, he picked her up in his arms and placed her in the middle of the bed. He took another *long* look at her curvaceous body before he started placing kisses all over it. With each kiss, he was rewarded with a moan. He hovered over her lips, wanting to kiss her, but refusing to do so. Their kisses were so intense, so passionate, that he knew the moment would move along even quicker if that happened. And he wanted to keep it slow so badly.

His perusal of her body was momentarily paused when her brown nipples hardened, begging to be suckled. He popped one breast in his mouth, kneading the nipple with his tongue. She cried out and jerked a little off the bed. He moved to the other nipple, repeating the same move and eliciting the same response from her.

"Please," she moaned when he started massaging her breasts. *"Please."*

He knew what she was asking for, but he wasn't finished yet. "There's so much more I want to do to you, Autumn Dupree."

"I know," she said with a sigh. "But my body is craving to have you inside me."

He closed his eyes at her words. Having a woman crave to have you inside her felt good. But having Autumn Dupree admit that she craved to have him inside felt pretty damn amazing.

She was already squirming underneath him and tugging at his boxers. He stood to remove them and save her the trouble. Then he walked over to his pants, found his wallet and took out one of two condoms he was glad he'd had sense enough to bring. She was watching his every move, licking her lips whenever he glanced at her.

"If you keep doing that, I may just take you up on your offer and skip the foreplay."

"If I don't feel you inside me *right now,* I may just have to do the honors myself because all I know is having you inside me is the only thing on my mind, and has been for weeks."

*Damn. She wins.* "You can't say shit like that to me and expect me not to react," he said as he joined her back on the bed. "I'm not just going slowly for you, I'm going slowly for me. I don't want to hurt you, and I've never desired to be inside anyone as much as I want to be inside you."

Her light eyes intensified, and before he knew what was happening, she was dragging his lips to hers. One flick of her tongue and he lost all ability to think straight. She may have kissed him first, but he took over the kiss within seconds. She'd successfully pushed him over the edge and he was drowning in her taste. Her scent. The fact that her legs were wrapping around his waist.

When he felt himself near her opening, he entered two fingers in her to see if she was wet enough. She bucked off the bed and moaned into his ear.

"Damn, Autumn. You are so wet."

"Tell me something I don't know."

He removed his fingers and she immediately moaned in disapproval. He planted himself back in line with her opening and gently began pushing himself inside her. She was so tight, and it took some effort to control his movements to ensure he didn't hurt her. When he was halfway in, he stopped to make sure she was okay. But Autumn wasn't having it. She lifted her hips so that he slipped in even more.

*Oh, crap.* If he survived the onslaught of pleasure ricocheting throughout his body, he had to make sure he remembered to tell her how much he enjoyed whatever movement she was making.

Minutes later, he was fully embedded in her body and the moment felt so surreal, he had to keep his eyes open to make sure it was really happening. She was still adjusting to his size, but he felt her body relax and when it did, he began to move.

"That feels amazing," she said when he increased his pace. "Don't stop what you're doing."

Oh, there was no way he was going to stop. Not until they both released the sexual tension that had been building for weeks. Maybe even longer than that. He didn't forget that she'd admitted the night in the alley had been her first orgasm brought on by oral sex or sexual intercourse. Had he known it had been her first orgasm, there was no doubt in his mind that he would have done something more special.

The louder she moaned, the more he increased the movement of his hips. He could tell she was getting close to having an orgasm. She just needed a little push.

He lifted her legs at an angle that he knew would hit her G-spot and knew he'd found it when she squealed and began to meet him pump for pump. She had been alternating between opening and closing her eyes, but now her eyes were open.

"Keep them open," he said as he slowed the rhythm of his hips so she could watch him thrust in and out of her. Some women weren't into that sort of thing and they'd rather just have sex and not pay attention to how it looked when their bodies connected. He took a chance that Autumn would enjoy it and he got her answer when fascination danced in her eyes.

"I think I'm close." Good. He wanted to watch her

face when she came, and there was no way he was missing it. After a slight adjustment, he increased his movements even more and felt his own desire threatening to spill over. But he wanted to wait until she had her experience first.

He didn't have to wait long. Within minutes, she let out a cry as her body convulsed and her vaginal muscles squeezed him, holding him hostage. Just the act alone of watching her release a strong orgasm was enough to push him over the edge. Usually he could gauge how strong his orgasms would be, but tonight, his judgment was off because his body jerked harder than he'd anticipated. Even as he came down from the high, he could still hear his own groan ringing in his ears. He fell to the bed beside Autumn.

*What the hell was that?* He'd never experienced anything that powerful before, and although he'd stuck to his limit and had only one orgasm, he definitely didn't feel in control of the situation. There was no doubt in his mind the minx lying beside him was the one holding his heart in her hand, and there wasn't a damn thing he could do about it.

# *Chapter 15*

His lovemaking was unforgiving. That was the only way she could describe it. Making love to Ajay was easily the most amazing thing she'd ever experienced. It demanded certain emotions from her body. Provoked feelings she'd never felt before. And even though she knew she should be nervous that he had such a hold on her mind and her body, instead she felt liberated. Uninhibited. Enlightened.

She glanced back at Ajay, who was walking behind her. In khaki shorts, a cream T-shirt and white-and-beige polo shoes, he looked good enough to eat. Either that, or she was still thinking about how good he looked naked.

After they'd had sex last night, he had spent the rest of the night massaging her body, collecting on the foreplay that she'd made him skip, causing her to have two more orgasms.

Earlier that morning, she'd found that she'd gotten only two additional texts last night. One from Danni and another from Summer. Both said they figured she was still with Ajay but reinforced the fact that both of them needed to meet the group for breakfast before the hiking competition. She'd confirmed they would both be there, but truthfully, she would have much preferred to stay naked in the bed with Ajay.

"What in the world made them pick a hiking competition?"

"What's wrong with hiking?" she said with a laugh. During breakfast, Ajay had been grumpy, and when she'd asked what was wrong he told her that he had wanted to stay in bed with her and continue what they started last night. It wasn't lost on her that he'd had only one orgasm, but she planned on changing that tonight.

"Nothing is wrong with hiking up a small hill, but there is nothing small about this mountain we're climbing. It's ninety-five degrees out here."

He was right. They had already been hiking for two hours. Winter and Taheim had thought it would be a good idea to separate them into teams of two and make it a competition. Along the hike, they had to find different-colored small flags and pick them up. The first team to the top with all ten flags won.

"We only have three more flags to get." He groaned at her comment. "How about we talk about something to take your mind off the hike? You put in a lot of work last night, so your body is probably just tired."

"Okay, let's talk, then."

"What do you want to talk about?"

"Um, let's talk about how sexy you look naked."

"I'm serious, Ajay."

"Me, too." He chuckled. "You look amazing in clothes, like these short blue-jean shorts and tank you're wearing. But you look breathtaking without a stitch of clothing."

She smiled even though he couldn't see her. "Thank you, but I mean it. Let's talk about something other than me being naked."

"If you insist. Hmm, let's see. Since being here, I've decided to be a guest speaker for a program in Chicago that aids women released from prison."

"Oh, really? How did you come to that decision?"

"My mom has volunteered for the program for over fifteen years."

"Wow. I swear, Mrs. Reed is so fierce. Love that about her."

"She is. She's been trying to convince me to speak at the program for years, but I always turn her down. My dad even called and asked me to speak a month and a half ago because he took my mom on vacation so she couldn't do it. But I wasn't ready to speak then. Being here has made me reevaluate a lot of things and do some self-reflection."

"I know what you mean. Bora Bora has had the same impact on me." She stopped walking and turned to face Ajay. "What does your mom want you to talk about?"

His face tensed. "My life growing up with a mother who was in and out of jail. The program isn't just for women released from prison. It's for their families, too. She thinks by sharing my story, I can help the kids."

"I agree. I think sharing your story with them is extremely brave and has the possibility of helping a child who is currently going through what you've been through. I'm proud of you."

"Thanks," he said as some of the tension released from his face. "I'm not brave. I'm just doing it to try to help others."

He looked as though he wanted to tell her more, but he was silent for a while. He seemed content to just stand there and look at her. She let him, hoping that she was giving him the support he needed.

"When I turned nineteen, I ran into my birth mom in our old neighborhood. Even though I hadn't lived there, I still went to visit my grandmother's friend, who was still living at the time. Immediately, I could tell she was strung out on drugs again. She looked a mess and she begged me to give her money. When I refused, she went crazy and started causing a scene right on the street. I gave her the money just to make her go away. Months later I heard that she got arrested."

She glanced around at the path they were on and motioned for him to sit next to her on a couple of large rocks. "What did she get arrested for?"

"For armed robbery, which she subsequently did to support her drug habit. I sometimes wonder if talking to her would have changed the outcome. Back then, I felt guilty for being adopted by the Reeds. I hadn't even thought about her that much until we saw each other in the street that day."

"She wasn't there for you like a mother should be. You can't be upset at yourself for moving on with your life and hoping for a better hand than the one you were dealt."

"I think that's another reason why I felt guilty. I've felt as if I was a part of the Reed family since I was seven years old. There's a lot that I block out from my past, but I know my past is what made me who I am today."

She picked up on words that he hadn't yet spoken aloud. "But there are some decisions you made in the past that you would change, right?"

"Exactly. Years later, I wish I could take back how I handled the situation when I heard she was out of jail and had been clean for two months."

Suddenly, she understood all too well the guilt he was probably carrying around. "What happened?"

He sighed and leaned his elbows back on the rock. "My mom had called me a few days after my twenty-fifth birthday to tell me that my birth mother was in the women's-aid program and she'd asked about me. My mom wanted me to talk to her and encourage her to stay clean, and build a new relationship with her. I went to the aid program that day and watched her through the window. She was waiting in the corner of the room and she looked so fragile. So broken. Years of pain and hurt reflected on her face. And I froze. I realized that I wasn't ready to talk to her. I wasn't sure what I would say or if I even wanted a relationship with her. I think I watched her from that window for ten minutes before I finally went back to my car."

As Ajay rehashed every emotion he felt as he looked through that window, her heart broke for him. He took a break and looked out at the trees blowing in the wind. "Two months after I saw her through the window, she overdosed. I never got a chance to make amends. Never got a chance to tell her how I felt or to figure out if she, too, wanted to make amends. I never got a chance to hear her side of the story and learn what happened in the years we'd been apart."

She hadn't even noticed tears had fallen down her face until she felt his hand brush them away.

"I already know what you're thinking, and I've never forgiven myself for losing out on the opportunity to speak with her one last time."

"That's not what I was thinking, Ajay." She wiped a few remaining tears. "My father always told me that you couldn't unring the bell. All you can do is move forward. That night it wasn't Ajay, the man, looking through that window. It was Ajay, the boy. The kid who had to grow up way too fast and saw way too much to be so young. You were frustrated. Angry. Hurt. Confused. She'd put you through hell and back and when you saw her through the window, all the emotions you felt came flooding back all at once."

"I didn't expect that to be the last time I saw her." His voice was so low she had to strain to hear him. "I was a grown-ass man, but I cried when my mom told me what had happened. The director of the women's-aid program had contacted her. I couldn't believe that I had missed two chances to make things right with her and I'd lost any chance of ever seeing her again. Mom and Dad didn't even ask me any questions about how I felt. They just consoled me and informed me that they were paying for my birth mother to be buried in the same cemetery as my grandmother. I've still never been there. Can't bring myself to go."

"Your parents really are amazing."

"They are. I don't deserve them.

"Yes, you do." She adjusted herself on the rock so she was facing him. "You've blamed yourself for years, but your birth mother made the choice to do drugs that night. I know you hate that you were never able to have an honest conversation with her, but you've carried this burden for ten years and you have to understand that even if you had spoken with her, the outcome may not have been different."

He dragged his long fingers down his face. "Trust me. I'm working on it. Speaking at the next program meeting is a big step for me, but it won't change the past."

"You're right, it won't. But it's definitely a step you need to take to start the process of forgiving yourself… and forgiving your mom. I, of all people, know how hard that can be. But I have faith in you, and as soon as you realize what an amazing man you are and understand that you can't let the past dictate your future, you'll be surprised at how much quicker the forgiveness process goes."

"Did you forgive your ex?"

"I'm still working on it. But I have forgiven my mom. I had to for my own sanity…"

He studied her eyes the way he had earlier, and just

like before, she sat there and let him get his fill. "I happen to think you're pretty amazing, too."

She felt her cheeks grow warm under his gaze. Separately, they had their share of problems, but together, she couldn't help but think there was anything they couldn't overcome. Opening up to Ajay was something she'd expected once she gave in to her attraction. Falling in love with Ajay wasn't the plan, but she had a feeling that was exactly where she was headed.

He leaned toward her and captured her lips in a kiss. She didn't know if it was possible, but each kiss seemed to be more passionate than the last. The only thing that would have been better was if they hadn't been sitting on hard rocks.

"You guys are never going to win that way."

Reluctantly, they broke the kiss. She lightly shook her head to clear away the lustful fog and spotted Jaleen and Danni standing a few feet away with big smiles on their faces.

"I don't know about that, Jaleen," Danni said, crossing her arms. "It all depends on if they are trying to win this hiking game or if they are trying to win something else entirely."

A witty remark was right on the tip of her tongue, but Ajay chose that moment to gaze into her eyes momentarily, cutting off all the oxygen to her brain. Not only did she read the look in his eyes, but they'd turned from light brown to deep gray. The change was taking her mind to a *very* naughty place. She wished she had the guts to ask him if he agreed with Danni. Were they playing for something else entirely? Was he playing for keeps or was she just his current fixation?

When his lips curled into a sexy side smile, she bit her bottom lip and moaned.

"I just need one more," he said before going in for another kiss, disregarding the fact that they had an audience. If anyone would have asked her months ago if she would have been sitting on a mountain publicly kissing the sexiest man she'd ever known, she would have laughed in the person's face. And now she wasn't sure she would stop the kiss even if ten more couples showed up to watch.

"Looks as though you're the lone wolf left in Chicago," Danni said, patting Jaleen on his back. "Better start planning single bachelor activities for one."

# *Chapter 16*

Autumn yawned and stretched her aching muscles. It was a good sore, but she definitely needed to take a bath sometime today. Last night, she'd decided to stay in Ajay's room. Jaleen and Danni had bragged about winning the hiking game all last night, leaving out the part about Ajay and Autumn letting them win.

The vibrant sunrise lit the dark room, reminding her that they would eventually need to shower and change for the day. She couldn't believe the wedding was tomorrow. They had the rehearsal and the rehearsal dinner, so the day would be packed with final wedding details.

She felt Ajay stir beside her and looked over to see if he was awake. *He even looks sexy when he sleeps.* She swore, the man didn't have an ugly bone in his body.

She brushed her hand down the side of his face before running her fingers over his abs. He stirred again, but he didn't wake up. The sheets were twisted around their bodies, but the most appetizing parts of Ajay were covered, and that just wasn't acceptable.

Oral sex had never been something she was really into, but she was realizing that with Ajay, she was enjoying a whole lot of things she didn't normally relish. The challenge that they'd agreed upon entered her mind. He'd successfully been knocking down the walls she'd built around her heart, and the past couple of nights he'd knocked down yet another as she'd experienced her first real orgasm through sexual intercourse. There was no faking it with Ajay. She didn't have to pretend to have a passionate release and then pretend to be asleep. With him, she could only give in to what she was feeling. Unleash the passion she'd always hoped was there buried deep inside.

Since she'd arrived on the island, she'd made a promise that she would enjoy herself without overanalyzing a situation. There was no room for overthinking in paradise.

She moved the sheet that was covering the part she was searching for and was surprised to see him enlarged. Clearly, even in his sleep, he had a high sex drive. She hesitantly moved fingers up and down his shaft, enjoying the feel of his skin rubbing against the palm of her hand. She stopped touching him long enough to move the rest of the sheets from his body. *Lord have mercy.* She didn't think she'd ever tire of seeing his magnificent body in all its naked glory. As she ran her hands over his muscular thighs, she got an idea of how she could collect on her end of the bet.

As carefully as she could, she eased his legs apart and nestled herself right in between both limbs. She wasn't positive, but it seemed as if his erection grew even more before her eyes. As if he knew what she was about to do. His body was still slowly rising and falling, so he was definitely still asleep. *Good. If you stay asleep long enough, I'll have you right where I want you.*

Ever so slowly, she eased her mouth over the tip of his erection and lightly sucked before sliding her tongue down one side of his shaft and then down the opposite side. She watched his face twitch, so she slowed her movements so that he would fall back into a deep sleep. When she was satisfied that he was back in dreamland, she continued her plan to please him to the point of no return. Since Ajay had a problem losing control in the bedroom and he was a lot stronger than she was, she knew she couldn't get away with doing whatever she wanted to him without him seductively turning the tables, as he'd done last night. She loved that he'd rather please her than please himself, but it was time for her to give back, and she was going to do so one lick at a time.

She got into a nice rhythm and figured it was time for her to add her hands to the mix. By the time he woke up, it would be too late for him to do anything about it, and he'd have no choice but to release the orgasm that he'd deprived her of last night.

Off in fantasyland, Ajay refused to wake up from the amazing dream he was having about Autumn. Dreams this good were meant to last, and even though he felt himself being tugged awake by sounds and noises that he couldn't understand, he refused to open his eyes.

He tried to stay in the moment and keep his dream alive, but the noises were really starting to bother him.

"Keep that, oh, yeah, there." *What in the world was that?* It sounded a lot like his voice, but he couldn't make out the words. *Maybe you should wake up...* He shook his head and ignored his thoughts. He didn't want to wake up. Men never woke up from great dreams like this. In his dream, Autumn was sexily kneeling in between his legs, sucking him so good, he couldn't help but wonder what she'd do when his dream turned to a reality. He usually didn't care for oral sex because he liked remaining in control. But for Autumn, he might reconsider, if the way this dream was going was any indication of how liberating it would feel to have her mouth on him.

In his dream, she increased the movements of her tongue and appeared to be trying to take him in whole, which was no easy feat. She started humming, and he didn't know if it was to drive him insane or make room in her throat for him. Either way, it was sexy as hell and he felt the pleasure all the way to his toes.

"Baby, what you do." *What the hell?* Once again, that gibberish sounded a lot like his voice. His entire body tensed and he started shaking his head from side to side. He was going to release himself, and the power of his orgasm was going to be forceful. More forceful than any orgasm he'd ever had in this position. He'd never recalled a dream feeling so real. So right.

*Shit, I can't hold back any longer.* Even in his dream he was trying to hold back, but Autumn's mouth was too demanding. His erection had grown considerably and her tongue hadn't eased up at all. *You have to wake up for this. Wake up!*

His hazy eyes flew open and the sight that he saw was absolutely breathtaking. Kneeling in between his thighs relentlessly sucking his erection and fondling him with her hands was Autumn Dupree. The woman who'd been the star of his latest dream.

He realized that the jumbled words he'd heard had actually been his. He felt caught off guard, and there was nothing gentlemanly about the way he was thrusting his hips into her mouth. Her eyes twinkled in amusement. She knew what she was doing and she knew there wasn't a damn thing he could do about it. He was already too far gone.

"Autumn," he said as a warning. He was on the brink and he couldn't stop it. Instead of slowing down, she sucked him even harder. He released a powerful orgasm followed by a range of grunts and growls that didn't even sound human. He was still convulsing from aftershock when he felt her hands on him again, only this time, she was rolling on a condom.

"What are you doing?" he asked when she began crawling up the bed.

She smiled slyly. "What does it look like I'm doing?" She straddled him and brought her mouth to his right ear. "Right now, I'm easing you inside me." And, oh, man, was she! It was the slowest entrance he'd ever experienced, and his erection was already sensitive from the orgasm he'd just had. His hands flew to her butt as she began moving up and down in a slow rhythm.

"If you want me to stop, then tell me right now." He heard her words, but he wasn't about to respond to them. There was no way he wanted her to stop what she was doing. He started rolling his hips to meet her movements.

"I'll take that as a no." With that, she briefly kissed his lips before leaning back up and slightly increasing her pace. When she dropped her head to the ceiling and placed her hands behind her on the bed, he made a mental note to see what other twists and turns she could do as a result of all that yoga she did.

Her breasts bouncing in front of his face looked too appetizing to leave unattended. He moved his thumbs in a circular formation over her sensitive nipples and was rewarded by a piercing moan that echoed through the spacious room.

She was so responsive, and not just sexually—although her moans were definitely becoming the sweetest song he'd ever heard. She was responsive when it came to everything they did and everything they were learning about one another. She didn't just offer advice and comfort when he discussed his past. She empathized with his pain. She shed tears of sadness for what he'd experienced. Everyone had certain fears they had to face, and every time he spoke to Autumn, she made him feel as though she wanted to be by his side to face them, as well.

When she finally leaned up and looked back down at him, he couldn't hold in his emotions any longer. He needed to switch their positions. Snaking an arm around her waist, he pulled her to his chest before gently laying her on her back, making sure he remained buried deep inside her.

She glanced up at him, her eyes a little uncertain. "Is this your way of stopping me from giving you another orgasm?" *She's so adorable.* That definitely wasn't the reason. He didn't want to express any serious sentiments in the act of making love, but he wanted to put her mind at ease, as well.

"In case you haven't noticed, I'm completely captivated by you, Autumn Dupree. So to answer your question, no, I don't plan on stopping anything." He watched the worry leave her features, replaced by the passion he'd been witnessing all morning.

His thrusts into her body were slow. Precise. Calculated. His eyes held hers as he tried to show her through his eyes what he felt in his heart. He'd often heard men say that they knew they'd found the one when they couldn't imagine their life without that person. They were great together. The perfect combination of a challenging and exhilarating relationship. He didn't know if she thought that anything that happened in Bora Bora would end here, but if she did she was sadly mistaken. He was fine with easing into dating, but he wasn't fine with being friends, and before they left paradise, he would make sure she knew that.

He grabbed her hands and placed her arms above her head as his thrusts quickened. Her labored breathing and the way she clenched her thighs were the signs he'd been waiting for. He was close himself.

He closed his eyes at the onslaught of passion flowing through his body. When he opened his eyes, a lazy smile was present on her face. It wasn't lost on him how monumental their moment was. Within seconds, she released a moan that he felt throughout his entire body. His own orgasm quickly followed, and was just as powerful as the first. The last thought to cross his mind as his spasms subsided was that Autumn had finally done it. She'd shown him what it felt like to lose yourself in someone else.

# *Chapter 17*

"What do you mean we aren't meeting up with the group?" Ajay was leading her to a boat and away from the main villa, where she thought they were meeting a few people for breakfast.

"I already told Winter and Taheim that we will be taking the morning off. They didn't mind as long as I promised to be back in time for rehearsal."

"Are you sure?"

"I'm positive," he said with a laugh. "Now get in this boat so I can show you your surprise."

She shivered, and it wasn't from the cool breeze that had just wafted through her hair. Normally, Ajay was the guy whom everyone ran to when they had a problem. He was strong. Kind. He cared about those he loved and there wasn't anything he wouldn't do for them. But he also had a dominating side that made her turn into a pile of mush when his voice grew all deep and husky. It was the same voice she heard when he released an orgasm loud enough to rock the villa.

She couldn't be sure, but it felt as if they were on a twenty-minute boat ride before a gorgeous green mountain came into view. Ajay got out of the boat first and lifted her out with ease. She followed him through a small crowd of people and down the dirt road to an open-window trolley that had a symbol and name on the side indicating that they were going on some type of tour. He held her hand as he led her to a couple of seats toward the middle.

"Are you going to tell me where we're going now?" she asked when the trolley began going uphill and passing an array of colorful plant life.

"You'll see soon," he said as he placed a soft kiss on her mouth. Convinced he wasn't going to give her a clue as to where they were going, she leaned into his arms to enjoy the beautiful view. Fifteen minutes later, the trolley stopped and passengers began exiting the vehicle.

"This is so adorable," she said as they walked through the small island village with a variety of souvenir huts, a couple of restaurants and a group of Polynesian dancers and singers entertaining the crowd.

"I thought we'd get off the resort grounds and experience more of the neighboring islands."

"I love it," she said, leaning up to plant a kiss on his cheek. "Where do you want to go first?"

"How about over there?" She followed the direction he pointed to and couldn't make out what it was. He led her over to a couple of men who were placing harnesses on a few other people.

"What is this?"

"This is the activity we're signed up for." He went to a man holding a clipboard and signed some paperwork. She walked over to glance over his shoulder right as he was signing the last page.

"Zip-lining! Where? We are practically at the top of the mountain."

"Exactly." He flashed her a sneaky smile. "We're zip-lining down the mountain."

Her jaw dropped and she looked around at the others seemingly excited about this adventure. "You've got to be kidding me."

"Are you afraid of heights?"

"No."

"Then, what's the problem?"

She studied his eyes, not sure if she had an answer for him. "I don't know. I just wasn't prepared to zip-line down a mountain today."

"Baby, you'll be fine." *There he goes calling me "baby" again.* How the heck was she supposed to focus when he spoke to her in such an endearing way? He pulled her away from the crowd.

"I know this isn't what you had in mind when I said I had a surprise for you, but I didn't want to tell you. I haven't told you this, but I'm terrified of heights. I don't even like roller coasters that go too high."

She squinted her eyes in confusion. "If you don't like heights, then why do you want to zip-line?"

He averted his eyes before peering back down at

her. "I never like losing control, but I lost control with you, and now I can't imagine being with you any other way. When you were in the shower, I called Winter and Taheim and asked for permission to skip the morning activities, and then I called the concierge desk and asked them to book this zip-lining tour. I've been experiencing a lot of firsts lately and I'm really enjoying this feeling… I don't want it to end, and I'd love to experience another first with you by facing my fear of heights."

She melted. Literally melted into a puddle of mush on the ground. Never had she *ever* heard someone talk to her so honestly. With Ajay, she didn't have to push him for more information or ask him to clarify how it felt. With Ajay, she just *felt*. She didn't want to lose that feeling.

Once they were strapped in, they both were secured onto the first zip line. During this round, two separate zip lines would be released at the same time, giving individuals the chance to zip beside their loved ones or friends.

"Are you ready?" she asked when the countdown began.

"Are you?"

"I'm ready for whatever you're willing to give." Those were the last words on her lips before they were released to fly through the canopy of lush trees. It felt amazing. So freeing. She heard Ajay yell and was able to glance over at him just as he pumped a fist into the air and extended his legs in front of him. They were in the air for only about fifteen or twenty seconds, but she had a feeling the impact of actually facing his fear of heights would offer hours of countless memories.

When they landed and were unclipped, they walked to the back of the wooden platform to prepare for the next round. Ajay had her in his arms within seconds.

"I can't thank you enough for experiencing this with me. I could *not* have done this without you." He squeezed her a little tighter. "Lately, there's not much in my life that I want to do without you. We just fit… As if we were made to fit perfectly together."

*Did I just moan?* If not out loud, she'd definitely moaned in her head. There was no denying it now. Absolutely no point in lying to herself. She'd fallen in love with Ajay Reed, and the thought brought tears to her eyes. At one point in her life, she hadn't known if she would ever experience true love. She didn't know how he felt, but even if he didn't feel the same way, she was glad that she'd allowed herself to fall for a man as amazing as Ajay.

"You're very welcome," she whispered as he continued to hug her. She could stand there hugging him forever.

They made it back in time for the rehearsal, although Ajay would have preferred to skip that, as well. He was excited for the wedding, and as sentimental as it sounded, he was even more excited to see the look on Taheim's face when Winter walked down the sandy aisle to join his hand in marriage.

Despite his excitement, his mind was occupied with thoughts of the woman walking down the beach with her arm linked to his and a bouquet in the other. It was hard to walk down the aisle and not imagine being in his brother's place one day. He had a feeling he wasn't the only one imagining that scenario.

He looked to his left and noticed Autumn's father observing them closely and wearing a smile. When they'd returned from zip-lining, they'd been informed that Autumn's father had arrived, and as soon as they were introduced, Mr. Dupree had wasted no time making small talk with him. He hadn't asked him too much; just enough to imply that he could tell he was interested in his daughter. Even though it was only a twenty-minute conversation, Ajay already liked him. He knew Mr. Dupree was French, but he hadn't imagined a six-foot-five man who looked a bit intimidating but was really easy to talk to.

His eyes gazed down at Autumn, and just as he'd hoped, she met his gaze as a soft smile formed on her lips. Movement in the corner of his eye caught his attention, and he looked over in time to see his parents share a knowing look.

The rehearsal lasted only an hour. It took only a few minutes after it ended for him and Autumn to get pulled in opposite directions. He didn't like it, but he understood that the entire reason they were in Bora Bora was to witness the union of Winter Dupree and Taheim Reed.

Now the rehearsal dinner was in full swing. The hotel staff had suggested they dine in a secluded private area of the resort grounds that sat mere feet away from the soothing water. Different groups were conversing with those in the section of their table, and Ajay was pretty sure he should be doing the same thing.

He wasn't being antisocial. He just couldn't keep up with all the conversations when the only person he wanted to talk to was seated ten people down from him. She was wearing a red sundress that dipped low in the front, and her curly hair was free and flowing in the wind. She looked gorgeous, just as she always did.

While he was getting dressed for dinner, he'd had a chance to think about how he would approach Autumn about continuing their relationship. Technically, they hadn't even had a conversation about being in a relationship, so maybe he should start with that. In his mind, they'd been together for months because somewhere along the line, Autumn had become the center of his thoughts…the center of his world.

Slow music began playing and couples began standing up from the table to dance. Ajay glanced around the room and noticed that everyone on the floor was either married, engaged or dating. All the singles appeared to be at the bar, flirting or talking among each other. As he excused himself from the groomsmen he was talking to, he began walking to Autumn. Her eyes followed his every step.

"May I have this dance?" He held out his hand to her. She placed her smaller one in his.

"Absolutely."

They hadn't shared a dance before, and even though Ajay enjoyed dancing, he'd never been into slow dances. At least, he hadn't been until he was dancing with Autumn. She felt perfect in his arms.

"I had a good time today. Thank you for surprising me."

"I'm glad you enjoyed yourself." That was an understatement. He was thrilled that she hadn't hesitated to embrace zip-lining after she realized how important it was to him.

"You've been surprising me since we met." She gave him a soft smile as she curled her arms around his neck. It was true. There was so much that he hadn't expected to happen. Her eyes were filled with so much emotion, and he knew he couldn't have been alone in his feelings.

He had to talk to her. He had to know if she was as interested in continuing their relationship in Chicago as he was. When she laid her head on his shoulder, his arms pulled her in tighter, closer. *I can't let her go.* He didn't want to even contemplate letting her go. Emotions this strong could only mean that she'd captured him in ways he never saw coming. He hadn't just fallen in love with her mind and body. He'd fallen in love with the person she rarely let others see. The woman whose soul and spirit matched his.

Later that night, he was able to spend more time with her. He wasn't sure how they'd managed to get alone time when the wedding was only hours away, but they had. With their hands linked, he followed Autumn down the deck of her villa to the stepladder that led to the lagoon.

"Let's get in." She motioned for him to follow her.

"You never cease to amaze me." When she'd told him she wanted to put on her bathing suit so they could take a dip, he hadn't expected her to want to take a dip in the lagoon when it was already dark out. He followed her to the ladder and they both waded into the warm water.

The light from her deck and his was enough to illuminate a portion of the water. She curled her arms around one of his arms as she looked around at the water.

"Just so you know, going into the ocean or any body of water that I know is home to a host of fish is one of my fears. Even more terrifying if it's dark outside."

He suddenly understood why she'd asked him to get into the water. He pulled her in front of him as he continued to tread water. He wanted her to feel comforted. Protected.

"Since I helped you face one of your fears, it seemed only natural that you help me face one of mine."

Her statement was true, but it wasn't accurate. She hadn't been helping him face one of his fears. He'd faced so much more than that. He felt her shiver, and began rubbing his hands up and down her arms.

"Are you ready to get in the plunge pool?"

"Oh, my God, yes," she said with relief. They were both still laughing when they slid into the plunge pool. Since Ajay could stand and Autumn still had to tread water, he used it to his advantage. He pinned her in a corner of the pool, and she immediately wrapped her legs around his waist. He dropped his forehead to hers.

"I love it when you do that," she whispered. "When you place your forehead against mine."

They closed their eyes as he breathed in her scent that had quickly become his latest addiction. He wasn't sure who opened their eyes first, but their lips mingled in a kiss that he felt all the way down to his toes. He didn't know if it was possible, but their kiss seemed to be filled with even more emotion than kisses they'd shared previously.

As their tongues tangled, demanding that they both give in to temptation, his hands roamed up and down her spine. She shivered beneath his touch, and her hips slowly, seductively began rolling her body over his groin.

Skilled fingers drifted to the string of her bikini top and untied the bow. The wet material eased down her breasts with her bikini bottoms quickly following. His swimming trunks were the next to be removed, and within seconds, he'd sheathed himself and positioned himself directly in front of her sweet spot.

His eyes were pinned to hers as he entered her in one *long* pleasurable stroke. There was no holding back when hc was with Autumn. He wouldn't even try. Being embedded deep in her core didn't just feel like he was coming home… It felt much deeper than that. As if he was laying a foundation for their future. A future full of hopes and promises.

He wasn't sure how she did it, but it always seemed as if she could read his mind and knew exactly what he was thinking. Her eyes danced with desire, and he was sure the feelings floating through his body were evident on his face, as well. He wished he could bottle up this moment and hold on to it forever.

# *Chapter 18*

There was nothing more perfect than witnessing a moment of true and undeniable love. As Autumn watched Winter and their father walk down the white sand beach, she couldn't help the tears that formed in the corners of her eyes.

They had been through so much as a family, and to see Winter so undeniably happy was truly the most precious moment. Winter's long A-line backless chiffon dress was a gorgeous snow white. The sexy lace V-neck and white-gold foot jewelry in place of shoes just added to the elegant grace of her look and style. It was hard for any of the attendees to take their eyes off her, especially Taheim, whose eyes watered as he watched his bride glide down the aisle.

The slight breeze in the warm weather and birds

flocking overhead were in perfect rhythm with the slight waves crashing on the shore of the beach. Nature was so in tune with the wedding that it seemed as if everything came together for this one special moment.

When her dad gave Winter away, he wiped the tears from his eyes before leaning in to kiss her cheek. He was giving away his eldest daughter, and even though he was giving her away to an incredible man, Autumn knew it was hard for her father. He was the strongest man they knew, and there were only a few who knew the struggles he'd had to overcome. But when it came to his daughters, Vail Dupree was a softy. Autumn glanced behind her at her sister Summer, who seemed to be trying to hold back tears just as hard as she was.

Once the guests were seated, she glanced at Ajay, not surprised to find him already watching her intently. She'd known he was watching. She could feel his gaze by the way her skin tingled with awareness. The way it always did when he was watching her. She'd been hesitant to look back at him for fear that she would be more consumed in watching him than observing the wedding. She brought her attention back to Winter and Taheim, but as always, her gaze slowly found his again.

It was amazing how one day you could be living a balanced life and then, without warning, someone could swoop in and knock you off your axis. That was what falling in love with Ajay felt like. Love was messy and demanding. It took hard work to make a relationship successful, and even then, love made no promises. What she'd learned by giving her heart to Ajay was that love may not have the ability to make promises, but it was a great foundation for building promises together. Promises that you would forever keep. Love may be challenging and at times overwhelming. But love was also worthwhile. Loving someone meant trusting a piece of your heart with the person and having the confidence that the individual would take care of it. Love meant finding a person who made you want to get up every day and fight to be a better person.

The hardest part of falling in love was not turning your back on it when you found your soul mate. Not allowing it to slip through your fingers because of past experiences. Everyone had his or her own definition of what it meant to fall in love, but for Autumn, falling in love meant entrusting that person with every single part of you. Knowing that once someone learned details about your past that impacted the person you are, the individual would stay with you and love you that much harder. Ajay was that for her.

She smiled as she thought of the couple they'd noticed at the wine bar a month ago. Never in a million years had she thought she'd experience what they had… but she did. She still was. Even from a short distance, she could see his eyes change color. She'd been around him enough to realize that they didn't just change when he was aroused or intrigued. His eyes also changed—deepened even—when he was filled with any type of emotion. It wasn't limited to just one feeling. The way he looked at her was so intense. So intoxicating. He consumed her in every way possible.

Her eyes went back to the happy couple as the officiant told Taheim that he could kiss his bride. There it was. There was that look of complete and utter satisfaction on their face as they were officially announced husband and wife.

The next forty minutes were filled with excitement and pictures as the bridal party gathered to congratulate Winter and Taheim before they headed to the chic beach reception.

"I'm so proud of you, sis," Autumn said as she pulled Winter into a hug after Summer hugged her.

"I couldn't have done it without the two of you." She wiped a couple of tears from her eyes. "Everything turned out so beautifully."

"It really did," Summer agreed. "The wedding could not have gone better. It's going to be hard for Autumn to top this."

"What do you mean?" she asked. "Why just me and not me or you?"

"Because I don't have a man like that," Summer said, turning her to face Ajay. "Staring at me as if I hold all the answers to his future."

Autumn glared at Summer because she'd said it loud enough for Ajay to hear. When she mouthed *sorry* to him, he said, "I'm not," loud enough for her to hear.

"She's right," Winter said when Autumn had turned to face her. "I know you don't do the whole wedding thing, but it's obvious how Ajay feels about you."

She felt it, too, but they hadn't really spoken about their feelings, or continuing their relationship when they got back to Chicago.

"I'm actually starting to think that weddings aren't that bad." Both Winter's and Summer's jaws dropped.

The conversation was soon forgotten as the other bridesmaids joined them and began sharing their favorite parts of the wedding. A couple of minutes later, the photographer had them get into position to begin taking the group shots. When Luke was positioned to stand right beside Autumn, Ajay quickly changed positions with him so that he was beside her instead.

"He was too close," he whispered in her ear. His breath teased her neck in a way that had her quivering on cue.

"You're not supposed to talk," she said between her clenched teeth. "You're supposed to be smiling."

He focused for about two more shots before she felt his gaze on her again. When she turned to tell him to focus on the photos, he tugged her into a sugary kiss before she could voice her words. The way that he kissed her was flawless...perfect in every way.

The reception was just as beautiful as the wedding, complete with elegant beach decor. The white linen tables were garnished with tea-light candles and teal sea glass. Three glass vases of different sizes containing white rocks, seashells and faux turquoise sea coral were decorated with pearl beads on wire garland. White or teal wooden signs stuck in the sand were used to show guests the direction of the sweets table, gift table, beach and other places they may want to check out. Crisp white material hung delicately across the tented section of the reception while white hydrangeas intermixed with native island flowers topped off the chic look.

Giving the best man speech had been a lot harder

than he'd thought. Taheim was so much more than a brother. Ajay often thought about what would have happened had Taheim not insisted on him coming over that day they met at the Boys & Girls Club. Taheim had found him once again at a time in his life when he'd felt as if he had no one. Would he have ever met the Reed family had it not been for Taheim? He'd like to think so, but it was unlikely. He owed Taheim everything…

Autumn's maid of honor speech hadn't left a dry eye in the place. They weren't just sisters; they were best friends.

Now that dinner was over, guests were either dancing or talking amongst each other. The sun would be setting in an hour and a half, and Ajay wanted to talk to Autumn before all the guests boarded a catamaran for the sunset cruise.

He searched the area and finally his eyes landed on her. She looked stunning in her knee-length chiffon turquoise dress that tied around the neck. The bottom of the dress swayed with even the slightest movement of her body. Selfishly, he wanted to steal her away from the people she was talking to, but she seemed to be enjoying herself. *Maybe I'll just wait to talk to her after the cruise.* He was pretty sure he knew how she felt, but what if he spoke with her and realized that she wasn't ready to enter a relationship?

"You know, staring at her isn't the same as talking to her."

Ajay turned around at the sound of his mom's voice. "I know that."

"If you know that, why haven't you taken Autumn

aside already?" He hadn't spoken to his parents about Autumn, but as usual, they always seemed to know things even if he hadn't voiced the words aloud.

"We haven't even discussed the possibility of being in a relationship when we get back to Chicago."

"Putting a title on your relationship is just a technicality."

"There's still more that we need to learn about each other before—"

"Once again, just a technicality. I understand, Ajay. You've never laid your heart on the line like this, and after what you've been through, your father and I understand. But Autumn is a tough woman, and whether you see it or not, you've already decided that she was worth your love and that you were worthy of hers."

He turned back to where Autumn was still standing. When she caught his eye, she winked and gave him a sweet smile.

"Are you afraid that she may not love you…or are you afraid that she does?"

His eyes flew to his mother's.

"Don't give me that look, Ajay. You've always given your dad, your brother, your sister and me a pass when it came to loving you because we knew you before your life got really complicated. However, for the women you dated in the past or the friends you let into your life, you've kept them at a distance and only told them what you wanted them to know. But I have a feeling with Autumn, you can't be that way."

He didn't want to tell his mom that he was fine with telling her how he felt. That wasn't what he was nervous about. He had so much more he wanted to suggest to her. If it were a simple "I like you, do you like me, too?" he wouldn't be standing there trying to figure out his next move.

"Moments ago, you were about to take her aside and tell her how you feel…so go do it."

He really didn't need any persuading since that had always been the plan, but he appreciated his mom limiting his procrastination. As he walked over to Autumn, no one else mattered but her.

"Can you join me for a walk?" he asked as he held out his hand.

"Sure." She placed her hand in his. He led her past a couple of onlookers and down a path that led to an isolated area that overlooked a tropical cove.

"This is gorgeous," she said softly when they arrived at the cove. Water drifted over black rocks as light waves broke gently on the shore. They walked barefoot on the soft sand until they arrived at a hammock that hung between two large palm trees. Even as he helped her into the hammock, he couldn't stop admiring her French-tip pedicure that she'd gotten that morning.

He sat and faced her instead of lying down. "You look breathtakingly beautiful."

"And you look incredibly handsome." She planted a quick kiss on his lips. "Is everything okay?"

"I just wanted to get you alone so I could talk to you before we went on the sunset cruise."

"What's wrong?" she asked as she placed her hand in his.

"Nothing's wrong," he replied as he brought her hand

to his lips and kissed her knuckles. "Unless you think that stealing my heart is wrong."

Her lips curled to the side. "I don't think anything is wrong with that. Especially since you stole my heart, too."

"You did more than steal my heart." He looked from their linked hands back to her eyes. "From the moment I met you, you challenged me in ways I never thought possible. From your suggestions for the menu at my lounge to the way your support encouraged me to share my story, you've been defying everything I ever thought about falling for a woman. It's always been hard for me to express myself and communicate my feelings, whether that be through words or actions. But with you, I find it easy to show you my affection in every type of way. My fear of being judged for decisions I made in the past or just my past in general… You've eliminated that by accepting me and understanding what I've gone through without passing judgment."

Her hand cupped the side of his right cheek. "But you did the same for me. My past is complicated, and even though I try not to let it define how I view certain things in life, I'm a work in progress… When I'm with you, I feel understood…respected…protected." Her lips briefly replaced her hand. "I know I'm not the easiest person to be around sometimes."

"Who is? Even when you give me a hard time, I'm completely enthralled by you. Being with me isn't easy, either, and there will be days when we will fight… But I can't imagine fighting with anyone else but you."

He gazed into her eyes and watched the emotion cross

her face. "You *get* me. Simply put, I can be myself around you. Instead of a suit-and-tie type of guy, I prefer classic urban wear and on more than one occasion, you'll catch me wearing Timberland boots over any other style of shoes. I'm not a shower-gel type of guy, but rather a bar-soap-and-water type of man. Soap and water isn't complicated, and I enjoy wearing just the right amount of cologne. I dislike clutter, but on occasion, I get sentimental and hold on to the strangest things."

His heartbeat accelerated. He took a deep breath before continuing, "When I'm around you, nothing else in the world matters. I've always hoped that I'd find someone I could spoil with kisses every morning and whisper words of affection to every night before bed. A woman I could come home to after a bad day who would comfort me without even having to know what happened. A woman who motivates me to want to be a better man…a better father for our future kids. A woman who would sneak into the shower with me when I least expect it and a woman who would let me love her unconditionally and know that my life is incomplete without her by my side."

Her eyes searched his, and he let her search them openly. "Autumn, there isn't anyone else but you. Never was and never will be. When you're in the room, I barely even notice anyone else is around, and when we're not together, I'm counting the seconds until I can be with you again. Simply put, I've fallen madly and deeply in love with you, Autumn Dupree, and I've been free-falling from the very start. I don't want my time with you to ever end. If I have my way…it never will."

* * *

*So this is what free-falling feels like...* Her breath caught in her throat. *He loves me... He. Loves. Me...* And the realization that he'd actually voiced the words she felt in her heart brought tears to her eyes. She shivered in excitement as strong emotions raced through her body.

"I've fallen in love with you, too, Ajay Reed. And not just the Ajay you are now, but the Ajay you were as a boy. The Ajay that had to grow up too fast and deal with more heartache than most."

She gazed into the uninhibited eyes of a man who'd completely stolen her heart with no plans of giving it back. "I don't think anyone in my life has ever understood me like you do. I'm the type of person who would rather do research on issues that are important to me than watch television. Libraries are often my favorite place to escape. I prefer wearing dresses and skirts to work because they make me feel sexy, although the occasional jeans and shorts are my clothing of choice. If I had a dog, there's no doubt that I would name her Genevieve after my grandmother whom I never got a chance to meet. My favorite color is yellow, but I don't wear a lot of it. Family means everything to me, but I've always been unsure if I will find a man who would truly love me. And not just surface love, but the deep kind of love that makes your toes curl just thinking about the way he feels about you."

She scooted closer to him as much as the hammock would allow. "You give me more than the toe-curling kind of love. With you, I feel as though I can truly be myself and I don't have to pretend to be someone I'm not. At times, it may be hard for me to open up, but when I'm with you, I find it hard to keep all my feelings bottled inside. Deep down, I knew the moment I met you that you were different. That you'd somehow impact my life in ways I didn't see coming."

Without warning, his lips found hers in a kiss that started off innocently, but transformed to a much deeper one. A kiss that held more promise and meaning than any kiss they'd ever shared. When he pulled back, she immediately missed having his lips on hers.

"That's not all." She read the vulnerability in his eyes. "I don't want to spend another moment apart. When we get back to Chicago, I would love for us to move in together. I don't care if it's my home or your town house. Or someplace else entirely. I just want us to be together so that we can continue to build on our relationship."

His eyes grew more serious. "I don't know how you feel about marriage and kids in the near future, but I want more than a relationship. I want a future with you. Someday soon, I want to get married and start a family of my own. I know we both still have issues from our pasts that we need to work out, but I can't imagine doing so without you by my side. Without you, nothing else matters."

Her heart swelled. This was it. This was the moment she'd been waiting for. The moment when she could vividly imagine a future with the man she loved. The feeling was so exhilarating, she had to briefly close her eyes before meeting his gaze again. "Then, you're in luck, because I can't imagine living the rest of my life without you by my side, either, and I want nothing more than to take the next step and start building our future together." She meant *every* last word.

# *Epilogue*

*Two months later...*

"Are you finished with your letter?" she asked Ajay as they sat at the kitchen table of his home. After Winter and Taheim's wedding, the pair had decided that moving into Ajay's home was the best option and they would lease out Autumn's town house.

Although it had been only a couple of months, living with Ajay had been nothing short of amazing. Within weeks, they'd fallen into a comfortable pattern and every day they were discovering something new they had in common.

"Almost," he replied with a deep sigh. One month ago, Ajay had kept his promise and had spoken at the women's-aid program for women who were released from prison and were trying to get their lives back on track. She'd gone with him that day, and even though she knew his story, hearing him rehash the details to the audience had been an emotional experience. After his speech, several members of different families had gone up to Ajay and expressed their gratitude for having him share his story. The entire time they were at the program meeting, Mrs. Reed had looked at her son as if she were the proudest mom in the world.

After that day, Autumn had heard about a new organization in Chicago called Born Again that held monthly inspirational meetings to teach people how to overcome obstacles and circumstances they may have been faced with. She'd asked Ajay to attend a meeting with her, and both of them were truly impressed by the organization. After speaking with the director, they learned that the members were people from all different walks of life who had gone through a tragic or trying period in their lives and ultimately wanted to start over. There were so many circumstances that caused people to join the organization, and the support that they were given was priceless.

Autumn and Ajay were slotted to speak at the next meeting and share their stories in hopes that it would help others who may have had to overcome similar obstacles. To prepare for the meeting, Autumn had suggested that Ajay write a letter to his birth mom about everything he would have said to her had she not passed away. At first, he wasn't receptive to the idea, since it was a letter she would never get the chance to read. So Autumn had decided that even though she wouldn't send her letter, either, she would write one to her ex in response to the letter he wrote her all those years ago. In her letter, she would mention all the reasons why she would no longer let that time in her life define her future.

Glancing over at Ajay, she knew he was the reason why she no longer carried around that burden. There were so many remarkable things about him, it was impossible to choose only a few things she loved. When he finished his letter, she took both of them and sealed them in an envelope together.

"What do we do next?" he asked when she placed the envelope in a small box.

"When the time is right, we will find a place to bury the letters. What we've gone through in our pasts isn't something we'll ever forget, and we shouldn't because it made us who we are today...and we connect on a certain level because of it. But we don't need to harbor burdens such as these, so by burying this box, we are saying that we are healing and moving on with our lives. No looking back. Only moving forward."

Ajay stood from the table and pulled her into his arms. "When did you get so smart?"

"You didn't know?" she said playfully. "Well, someone should have told you before you fell in love with me."

His eyes glinted with amusement. "Something tells me I would have fallen in love with you regardless. You're pretty damn incredible."

Her gaze bounced between his eyes and his lips. "And you're absolutely amazing." Just then, the newest addition to the household squeezed her way in between them and started barking.

"I think Genevieve agrees," she said as she glanced at the eight-month-old puppy holding her red leash in her mouth. When they'd found her at a nearby animal shelter, both Ajay and Autumn had immediately fallen in love with the dark brown Labrador.

"I better take her for a walk," Ajay said before placing a sweet kiss on Autumn's lips that she felt deep in her soul.

"Okay, I have to meet the girls for yoga, so I will probably be gone by the time you get back."

As Ajay placed the leash on Genevieve, Autumn went to the front closet to grab her gym bag and put on her shoes. Ajay was almost out the door when he glanced back to Autumn, who was still at the closet.

"Is that new?" he asked as he pointed to one of the items she had in her hand, but she wasn't sure what he was pointing to.

"Is what new?"

"The yoga mat."

"Oh, yeah," she said, using the attached strap to sling it over her shoulder. "I saw it in the store the other day and fell in love with the motivating words written on it."

"Hmm… It's nice, but I like your purple-and-black one more. You look so sexy when you work out on it."

Autumn froze. She hadn't used that mat in front of Ajay yet. When she did yoga at home, she used her simple black mat that never left the house.

"When did you see me use my purple-and-black

mat?" His sly smile told her all she needed to know. "Did you see me working out that day on the beach?"

"If you're referring to the time when you were spying on me in Bora Bora, then yes, I saw you working out that day."

"Then, clearly you had been spying on me first." She placed one hand on her hip.

"I was running and spotted you doing yoga," he admitted. "When I noticed you were wrapping up, I decided to leave before you noticed."

"So you pretended that you were still running by the time I saw you?"

"Pretty much," he said with a laugh. "I was hoping you followed me."

"So that you could strip in front of me? Why didn't you say anything? I was crouched down in the plants like a stalker."

"At first, I thought about saying something. But it was way too funny watching you try to spy on me. By the way, you're no Sherlock Holmes. I heard every branch you stepped on, and if that wasn't loud enough, I heard your moans of appreciation, too."

"I did not moan!"

"Oh, yes, you did. I liked it, though. Gave me an opportunity to see how far you would go when you thought I wasn't paying attention."

She smiled as she began shaking her head in disbelief. "I can't believe I thought you couldn't see me that day. That's so humiliating."

"No, it isn't," he said, pulling her to him while still holding the leash in his hand. "You were adorable that day. I tried to prolong removing my clothes as much as possible just so that you wouldn't leave."

She squinted her eyes. "You know I'm getting you back, right? And you shouldn't bother preparing yourself because it will be when you least expect it."

His eyes went from playful to serious in a matter of seconds. "With you, I'm learning that I should always expect the unexpected. And if I'm not mistaken, you're learning the same thing." A cunning smile slowly spread across his face. She knew that look. She'd fallen in love with that look. Ajay Reed had something planned, and she had a feeling that she knew what it was. She didn't know when. She didn't know how. But she knew in her heart that they would be taking another step in their relationship very soon...and she couldn't wait to see what happened after that.

* * * * *

HARLEQUIN®
A Romance FOR EVERY MOOD™

SPECIAL EXCERPT FROM

*After dumping her controlling fiancé, Chey Rodgers is ready to live her life. Step one is moving to New York to complete her degree—getting snowed in with a sensual stranger isn't part of the plan! Successful attorney Hunter Barrington has one semester to succeed as a professor at his alma mater. He's put to the test when the sultry beauty who shared his bed at a ski resort reappears in his classroom. Will Hunter and Chey be able to avoid scandal and attain their dreams of each other?*

*Read on for a sneak peek at*
*HIS LOVE LESSON, the next exciting installment of*
*Nicki Night's*
***THE BARRINGTON BROTHERS** series!*

"Nice seeing you again…um…?" She pretended to forget his name.

"Hunter," he interjected and held his hand out once again.

Chey shook it and that same feeling from before returned—a slight flutter in her belly.

"Well—" she cleared her throat "—have a good night. I guess I'll see you around."

"I'm sure. Probably right here in the same spot." He chuckled.

"Oh. Sorry," Chey said for lack of anything better. "Good night," she said again.

HKMREXP0416

Chey didn't stop walking until she reached her villa. She pushed the door open, then quickly closed it behind her and leaned her back against it. Why was her heart beating so fast? Why was she flustered? Chey had carefully planned out her day and now that she'd had another encounter with the stranger—Hunter—she was mentally off balance.

Shaking off the feeling that had attached itself to her from the moment he touched her hand again, Chey headed to the first bedroom and pulled out her laptop. She decided to work on her novel. She booted up her computer and started reading through the last chapter she'd written. Every time she read the male character's lines, she imagined Hunter's voice, until finally she put the laptop aside and burst out laughing.

Chey lay back on the comfortable bed and savored the firmness of the mattress as it seemed to mold itself to her body. A vision of Hunter sleeping uneasily in that chair in the lobby popped into her mind. Chey closed her eyes tight in an attempt to rid herself of thoughts of him. She worked at this for some time before rising from the bed, bundling up and heading back to the main reception area to find Hunter, who was now "resting" in a new chair.

"You can have the second room in my villa on one condition."